the
bad boy
bargain

the
bad boy
bargain

KENDRA C. HIGHLEY

Entangled Publishing, LLC
2614 South Timberline Road
Suite 109
Fort Collins, CO 80525
Visit our website at www.entangledpublishing.com.

Crush is an imprint of Entangled Publishing, LLC.

Edited by Heather Howland
Cover design by Heather Howland
Cover art from Shutterstock

Manufactured in the United States of America

First Edition November 2016

For my daughter

Chapter One

Badass, troublemaker, girl magnet—familiar words always followed Kyle from his locker to his senior English classroom. Or from the cafeteria to the parking lot. Or from the locker room to the baseball field. Anywhere he went, the whispers followed.

Today, it went something like, "Ooh, I know who we should vote most likely to drop out before graduation," as he walked by. Or, "I heard he banged two girls at once at North Texas last weekend. College girls, man!" Or, "Dude, I heard MLB scouts are coming to the games to watch him play."

He wished that last one were true.

Kyle zipped his hoodie up tighter, acting like he couldn't hear a word. The dark red hoodie and a pair of headphones were pretty thin armor, even if he did encourage the stories… the lies. Suttonville High was a big enough maze of suck without letting the truth out.

And no way, no how, was he showing any sort of weakness

ever again.

"Dude! Wait up!" a guy called.

For a second, Kyle stiffened. Old habits died hard. But he recognized the voice and let his shoulders relax. Cade Adams, unlike the hundreds of rich, snobby kids crowding the halls, was worth waiting for. He slowed his stride until Cade caught up, looking disheveled. For an amused moment, he wondered if Cade was running from a pack of zombified football players, then he noticed the pleading look on Cade's face. The same one he'd ignored from a half dozen other guys.

He shook his head. "Nope, still not going."

"It's supposed to be a great party," Cade said, running a hand over his hair to coerce it back into shape. It was a little too long, and curls kept springing up on his head. "First night of spring break, man. All the seniors are going."

"Everyone except me," Kyle said, quickening his pace.

"Come on," Cade pleaded. "I *need* to be your wingman. Just once. Your leftovers would be a feast to us mere mortals."

That's what half the baseball team said, too. But if he let someone be his wingman, they'd find out really quick that he wasn't what everyone assumed. "Sorry, not my scene."

"Fine. Okay, I get it." Cade's crooked smile didn't do much to hide his disappointment. "Just…think about it."

He strode off, breezing through the hall filled with students in designer clothes as if his *Iron Man* T-shirt, wild hair, and faded jeans didn't matter to him. And it didn't—at some point last fall, Cade had become cool. Either that, or he'd stopped caring what any of them thought.

Lucky bastard.

Kyle stalked to chemistry, praying he'd pass today's test. Being dyslexic turned the periodic table into a medieval torture device, even if his teacher was good about giving him tutoring on the down low. He couldn't let anyone know he actually *cared* about his grades, aside from passing to play baseball.

"I heard he's going out with some girl at Texas Woman's," a girl whispered to another as he walked in, as if he couldn't hear them.

"Wish I knew for sure if anyone here has a chance," said the other girl, a pretty senior who had a reputation of being a man-eater. "Because I'd ride that pony all over town."

Kyle's ears flamed up. To hide his discomfort, he rolled his neck, getting a little satisfaction out of the wary stares after the vertebrae cracked. That's right, the scary kid just *cracked his back*. You puny humans shouldn't try that at home.

The bell rang and he sank into his desk, adopting his typical pose of "I'm only here because the truant officer made me show up today" with his legs stretched out in the aisle. Mrs. Moody, the chem teacher, rolled her eyes. She saw right through him. And if she could, how much longer would it be before everyone else did?

During the test—in which chemical compounds morphed into ancient Hebrew right before his eyes—he couldn't shake the conversation with Cade. He felt bad about letting the guy down, especially since he hadn't been much of a friend the last few years, but he hated those parties because of the baggage that rode on them. Namely, his reputation.

Because who at Suttonville would believe that the resident delinquent, skateboard-riding, drag-racing, smart-mouthed chick magnet Kyle Sawyer was actually *none* of those things?

Chapter Two

FAITH

"Faith Gladwell?" The school secretary's voice was bored. "Your mother left you a package."

Faith sighed in relief. She hadn't meant to leave her ballet shoes at home, but she'd nearly been late for first period, and a tardy on her record was worse than the shame of calling for help.

She took her dance bag from the secretary and flashed her a big smile. "You made my morning."

Like magic, the secretary smiled back. "Glad to help."

That was thing most people missed about life—being nice actually worked. And with a name like Faith Gladwell, people *expected* nice. They wanted an angel with a sweet smile and bubbly attitude, and she was happy to oblige. Most of the time, anyway.

But it was getting harder. Wings were heavy and really hard to keep from dragging on the ground. Especially when you dated one of the most popular guys in school—and you weren't sure you wanted to be with him anymore.

She hurried to the drama room, dodging past other students as if it were all a dance. Everything was a dance to her, especially now with her big break on the horizon. The musical was in two weeks, and they'd be starting dress rehearsals soon. After Mr. Fisk had learned she was classically trained in ballet, tap, jazz, and hip-hop, he'd insisted she try out for the lead in *Oklahoma!*

"You're a triple threat, dear," he said in his drawling theater voice. "We knew you could sing, and you can certainly act...but you can dance? Well, between all that and your girl-next-door demeanor, and you're perfect for Laurey. I can just see you pirouetting in the dream sequence. Perfect!" He'd snapped his fingers and strode off, shouting for the costume designers to come take her measurements, not even waiting for tryouts to be finished.

The lead...she still couldn't believe Mr. Fist had picked *her*. Mom was thrilled. Dad had taken to singing "The Surrey with the Fringe on Top" at random intervals. Even her older sisters had called home to say congrats.

Cameron, though, had frowned and asked how much time the rehearsals would take up. "Will I be able to see you?" he'd asked. "Or will the musical take up all your time?"

Some people would call that sweet. Faith called it "smothering slowly," especially since she knew he wasn't really missing *her*, but a warm body to coo at his football stories and let him stick his hand up her shirt. She'd almost told him, nicely, that he could keep himself perfectly good company, given what he really wanted out of her.

So much for nice.

She hummed as she skipped through the halls. Getting the lead in the school musical was one more box checked for her high school bucket list. Only two marks left:

Get accepted to NYU's musical theater program.

Have sex with a guy she loved.

Her mother would need smelling salts if she ever peeked in Faith's diary, but what she didn't know wouldn't give her a stroke. Dad? Well, he'd lock her up and go shopping for chastity belts.

Faith snorted. That image was way too easy to conjure up. Dad probably knew someone who made chastity belts. He hadn't even let her get into a car with a boy alone until she was sixteen. S-E-X wasn't spoken of.

Faith slowed in front of the drama room, feeling a little pang catch her heart. Her family loved her. They loved her dreams, her dramatic streak, and even her feet, ugly from years of dance. Still, she knew they worried about her. The baby. The one most likely to turn out wild.

And they *hated* Cameron.

Funny thing was, she was starting to see why. Every time they went out now, his hands got a little more aggressive, and he couldn't understand why she was reluctant to go past second base after dating for six months.

She didn't have the heart to tell him it was because she was waiting until she really fell in love…and that she didn't love him.

God, that was going to be a horrific conversation, wasn't it?

"Faith! Wait up, you long-legged gazelle!" Violet Moore dashed after her, cursing the fact—loudly—that she was five three and friends with a girl who was five nine. "George Washington on a pogo stick, you walk fast."

She chuckled. Violet's ponytail was coming lose from its elastic and her face was red. "How long have you been trying to catch me?"

"Since you left the office!" Her best friend paused to suck down air. "I wanted to make sure you can still meet after school to get ready for the party."

"Yep. I'll be there at three thirty."

"Good, because I'm seeing my hair stylist at five."

Faith's eyes widened. "You're really going to do it?"

Violet swung her ponytail. "Hell yassss. Tell your mom we'll send her the hair for the foundation."

"Sweet!" Faith grinned. "I can't wait to see you with short hair. It'll match your height."

"Aw, shut up, Amazon." But she smiled. The smile faded fast, though. "Great. Asshat at eleven o'clock."

"Cameron?"

"Yeah. I'm going to blaze before I say something that'll land me in jail." Violet gave her arm a squeeze. "You need to turf him. And soon."

"I know." She sighed and turned. Cameron was muscling his way past a group of freshmen to get to her. "I'll…I'll do it after the party."

"Good girl. Later!"

Violet left a vapor trail, racing away before Cameron reached Faith. "Why'd she run off?"

"Class." Faith hid a cringe. "She was asking me to help set up for the party."

"Getting the weekend started right!" he crowed, throwing a possessive arm across her shoulders and pulling her against his side. "You'll be ready at eight, right?"

"Yeah." Her heart sank. "I'll be ready."

Chapter Three

The ball came hurtling down in a perfect arc toward left field. Tristan yelled that he had it, but Kyle waved him off, running hard and laying himself out flat to catch it. The front of his body slammed into the grass and slid, but he cupped his mitt around the ball. "Got it!"

"Sawyer, save the diving catches for games, okay?" Coach Swanson yelled. "That goes for you, too, Murrell! That ball was Sawyer's, and I don't need any heroes on the practice field!"

Tristan rolled his eyes, grinning as Kyle peeled himself off the turf. "Nice grass stains."

Kyle looked down. The front of his practice jersey was one big swipe of green. Just the way he liked it. "You know me. Not happy unless I'm filthy."

"That's what all the girls tell me!" Tristan called as he drifted back to his spot about sixty yards away.

Kyle pretended to brush dirt off his knees to hide his

flush. "What's your mom say?"

"Bastard!" But Tristan's tone was cheerful. "What, you gonna marry that ball, or throw it?"

Kyle stood, noticing their pitcher was waving at him. Kyle wound back and threw it past his cutoff man at shortstop, straight into the pitcher's waiting mitt. The shortstop tossed up his hands. "Dude, I'm *right here*. Stop throwing past me!"

"Batting practice!" Coach shouted, and the assistants herded them all to the dugout. "Sawyer, you first, since you seem to have some pent-up energy."

Tristan opened his mouth to make some other smart-ass remark, but Kyle grabbed his bat and headed to the batter's box before he could say anything. Sure, he had a rep to protect, but it got old, listening to all of them talk about his "love life" as if it were a legend in the making. It made his insides squirm, knowing how hard they'd laugh if they knew it was just that: an urban legend.

He swung his bat a few times, then stood ready, waiting for the pitch. A slider, a little high. Kyle let it go by. "Ball!"

"Oh, shut up, Sawyer."

When the pitcher wound up again, Kyle knew it would be a fastball, probably low, but not too low to swing at. The ball came flying toward him, and Kyle swung with full power.

Crack! God, how he loved that sound. The ball sailed over the pitcher's head, and it had good distance. It flew over the fence, and the guys on the bench groaned.

"Home run," Coach said. "Dennings, throw him a changeup. That fastball was a grapefruit, kid."

Kyle stepped back into the batter's box, waggling the bat a bit. Knowing it was a changeup didn't help. He had to see it, understand the trajectory, before he could decide to swing.

The guy wound up, then threw. Kyle saw it go wide and turned his body. The ball smacked into his hip, sending a bolt of numbness down his leg.

"Sorry," Dennings said. The sheepish expression on his face was more than enough to let Kyle know it wasn't on purpose.

Coach let Kyle take a seat after that, sending a sacrificial freshman up for a turn. Tristan turned to him as soon as he sat down. "You going to Vi's party tonight?"

Kyle shook his head. "Other plans, man."

"Please tell me it involves a couple of college girls and a pillow fight."

"I don't talk." He raised an eyebrow at Tristan. "I like to give you guys something to wonder about."

"Must be something good." Tristan heaved a sigh. "Wish I could come with."

Kyle snorted. His *date* was with a lawn mower. He doubted Tristan would find that exciting. "Sorry…this is a one-man job."

And, for as long as he could keep the con running, that's all it would ever be.

The sound of a lawn mower wasn't a song of boring chores. No, it was his future. Kyle smiled as Avenged Sevenfold blared through his earbuds, barely drowning out the Toro's motor. He loved spring…and he loved the work that came with it. He might not get the periodic table, but he could turn someone's lawn into a green carpet of awesome.

His dad called it a gift. Kyle couldn't disagree. He understood plants better than people sometimes, and definitely more than words that rearranged themselves on the page without warning. If anyone at school figured out his love of gardening, though, he'd never hear the end of it. That's why he drove the black Charger his grandpa had given him for his seventeenth birthday to school, and why his beloved

Toyota pickup with ninety thousand miles on it stayed hidden inside their six-car garage so their snobby neighbors wouldn't complain.

He laughed as he made a turn around the Denkhoffs' lawn. They had great grass, and a big-ass yard surrounding their big-ass house. He could charge thirty bucks to mow it and Mrs. Denkhoff didn't even bat an eyelash. None of his customers did, not when they found out he could work a form of alchemy that resulted in "best lawn in the neighborhood" awards and the envy of their neighbors.

The air had a little bite to it, but he could tell it would warm up fast this week. March was always like that in North Texas. Some years it was fifty degrees and raining. Some years it was ninety degrees and humid as hell. From the blue sky above, Kyle knew the weekend would be gorgeous, probably low eighties and sunny.

He had pushed the mower around the bend at the side of the house when the lady next door waved at him. She looked vaguely familiar…wait—she was the woman in those TV ads about the children's cancer center. That's right—she ran the Gladwell Foundation. Dad was a fan and donated money to it every year.

He powered down the mower and took out his earbuds. "Did you call me, ma'am?"

"Are you Kyle?" she asked, breathless.

She stood atop the retaining wall between the yards, making him crane his neck to look up at her. God, he hadn't broken one of their sprinkler heads or something, had he? "Yes, ma'am?"

"Thank goodness. Sherry tells me you're good with yards. I'm having a benefit tea in my backyard in a month, and we have some serious problems with our grass back there. Well, that's not true. We have serious problems with *everything* back there." She smiled. "I'm Michelle Gladwell, by the way. I think you go to school with my daughter? Faith?"

If he did, he didn't know her. There were seven hundred students in his senior class. Kyle shrugged. "Yeah, I guess we do."

"So, would you have time to take a look? At the grass I mean?"

He barely choked back a laugh. What, was she worried he thought she meant Faith? *Sorry, lady, your daughter's virtue is safe with me.* "Is tomorrow morning okay? It's already getting dark, but I have plenty of time to get started this weekend."

"That's perfect."

After letting her know he'd be by around ten to give her an estimate, he cranked up his music and started the mower again. He usually avoided customers with kids who went to Suttonville with him, but it probably didn't matter. It wasn't like he'd see much of Faith anyway, and so what if she told people he mowed lawns? You could still be a badass and have a job, right?

Maybe he should've taken up auto repair. Dad had insisted he get a job that required manual labor. The piles of homework, the long hours of baseball practice, and the trust fund didn't matter. His father believed in hard work.

"Son, I don't care if you don't have to work for a living… ever," he'd said when Kyle turned thirteen. "There's value in seeing how everyone else lives—and everyone else has a job. So figure out what you like to do, and do it."

The very next day, he'd offered to mow Mrs. Perkins's lawn. She was eighty, stone deaf, and the richest widow in the neighborhood. It had taken him four hours to learn how to work the mower and edger and finish the job. When he was done, she'd given him five bucks and a pat on the head. He'd stared down at the five-dollar bill like it was a Franklin, and even now pride rose in his chest at the memory. He'd finished the job, on his own, and had proof he could do something right.

He started mowing for her every week after that. Soon he was mowing her friends' lawns, and branching out into full landscaping work.

Now he owned a pickup truck with one of those magnetic decals on the side: Hard Rock Landscaping. He even had a business cell phone.

If anyone at school figured out just how seriously he took his work, it would ruin his image. Better to let them think it was community service for a misdemeanor, because Kyle Sawyer, the trust-fund gardener, sounded much less cool than Kyle Sawyer, the delinquent.

And he needed to hold on to that image. He wasn't going back to being that weedy, picked-on eighth grader. Not ever again.

Chapter Four

The doorbell rang five minutes early. Cameron was never, ever early.

That wasn't a good sign.

Faith rushed to finish her mascara as Mom called, "Honey! Cameron's here!"

Her palms grew damp with sweat, and her stomach turned over. The party was going to be great, sure, but how could she go with him knowing she wanted to end it? Could she tell Cameron she was ready to move on? That she was tired of hearing about football, tired of how his hands always drifted toward her ass when he put an arm around her waist?

She knew she'd been lucky; at least she'd felt that way when he asked her out the first time. That he'd noticed her. She wasn't a cheerleader or blond or ultra popular. And in the beginning, he'd been almost perfect. Almost. But once he'd gotten comfortable, things had changed.

She wiped her sweaty hands on her denim miniskirt,

taking one last glance in the mirror. Her dark hair framed a pale face, making her brown eyes stand out, almost black, and she was trembling. God, he'd know as soon as he saw her that something was wrong.

"Faith?" Mom sounded vaguely worried. "You coming, sweetheart?"

"Be right down!" There, her voice sounded normal, right? To steel herself, she stared at her costume for the ballet scene in *Oklahoma!* Thinking how she had a lot in common with Laurey steadied her nerves. Laurey stole a wagon from Jud when he tried to paw her, knowing all he saw was a girl to conquer. Not someone to love, to cherish.

That's what Faith wanted—if she was going to give everything to a guy, he better damn well cherish the heck out of her. He should make her breath hitch when he walked into a room. His smile should warm the air. Make her feel like she was the only being in the universe.

He shouldn't spend entire dates retelling the story about how he caught the winning touchdown against Allen High junior year.

Taking a deep breath, she flung her bedroom door open and marched down the stairs. The first thing Cameron did was take a good, long look at her, up and down. Maybe she should've worn an overcoat instead of the miniskirt, leggings, and striped cardigan over a tank top. Not much skin showed, but he found every last bit of it.

A month ago, two, and that appreciative stare would've made her laugh. Tonight, though, it made the hairs on the back of her neck rise, and not in a good way.

What would she give for a guy who could do that—make her shiver…and enjoy it?

Instead, she trudged over to Cameron. He looked like someone you'd find on a poster for one of those high school football dramas. A *Friday Night Lights* golden boy, from his dirty-blond hair to the navy-and-gold Suttonville High letter jacket he never took off—especially not on a March evening with temperatures in the upper sixties. She'd even seen him wear it in September, when it was a hundred and two degrees and the devil had left the barn door open to hell. Who wore a letter jacket year-round in North Texas? You barely needed a coat in *January* half the time.

"Um, Faith?" he asked, smiling a little. "You in there?"

She jerked out of her thoughts and forced a smile in return. "Sorry. Just thinking."

"That'll get you in trouble."

Bojangles, her cat, rounded the door into the entry and hissed at Cameron. He hissed back.

Faith frowned. "Quit stirring him up."

He laughed, cocky and sure. "That cat hates me."

Well, yeah, Cameron ruffled Bojangles's fur up the wrong way every time he petted him. Cats hated that. "He's the alpha. You're in his space."

"Fine. I'll leave the demon-cat alone." He opened the front door for her. "Bye, Mrs. Gladwell!"

"Back by midnight!" she called from the kitchen.

Luckily Mom didn't see the brief look of annoyance on his face. He led Faith down to his F-150—bright red—and said, "I swear, she treats you like you're five. Who has a curfew anymore?"

She slipped into the passenger seat. "I have to be at the studio at nine tomorrow. It's just her way of reminding me I need some sleep. Teaching a group of wiggly first graders how to plié takes patience, you know."

He didn't answer, and they drove in silence out to the Moores' place. Violet's house was on the lake, with a huge backyard and a fire pit. Her best friend's parties were legendary, and they'd both worked so hard to make everything perfect, hanging paper lanterns, dragging out all the coolers, and setting up lawn chairs.

They turned down the oak-lined road near Lake Sutton Estates. The branches swayed in the twilight sky, and the air smelled like spring, green and new. Like an ancient hibernating nymph reborn in a sea of bluebonnets.

"I'd give five bucks to know what you're thinking." Cameron's hands tightened on the steering wheel. "You look gorgeous, by the way."

If she told him she was thinking about bluebonnets, fairies, and being reborn, he'd laugh. "That I love spring."

"Yeah, me, too." He reached out and rested his hand on her thigh. "Makes me horny."

Faith pushed his hand off her leg. "That's not what I meant."

"Yeah, I know," he muttered.

"What?"

"Nothing." He drove the truck through the gate at the end of Violet's driveway. Dozens of cars were already parked all over her front yard, except for a spot right by the gate—that one had a sign that read: MY BESTIE PARKS HERE. YOU'VE BEEN WARNED.

Faith grinned. Violet hadn't said she was saving them a spot. "That was nice of her, don't you think?"

"Sure."

His flat tone made Faith uneasy. "What's going on?"

"I should ask the same thing." He got out of the truck without waiting for her.

She clambered out after him. "What's gotten into you?"

"Can you answer the same question?" He stared at a point over her head, but when she didn't answer, his eyes found hers. They were hard, and a little hurt. "Thought so."

He took off for the gate. He'd just given her the chance she needed, and she hadn't dug up the courage to tell him. She couldn't let him walk away. Not now. "Are you even going to stay here and talk about it?"

"No." Cameron turned to look at her over his shoulder. "I'm going to get a beer."

With that, he disappeared through the gate, leaving her alone in the dark. For a minute, she let hurt tears rise in her eyes before getting pissed with herself. If he wanted to run off and have a beer with his friends, whatever. She'd find him before the night was over, tell him she was done, and ask Vi to drive her home later.

She shoved her way through the wrought iron gate, greeted by heavy bass pumping out of the speakers mounted on the patio. People were sprawled out on chairs, or dancing, or slipping away into the dark to hang out by the lake. There was no sign of Cameron—he'd already blended in.

"Dah-ling!" a girl called in a fake British accent. "You look smashing this evening."

Faith laughed and turned. Violet was teetering on enormous black wedges, wearing a dress that could only be described as flapper chic. Fringe…so much fringe. "Oh my God, your hair!"

"You like?" Violet turned in a circle. Her hair, a shining black pixie cut with purple streaks, shone in the firelight.

"Yeah. I'm just…surprised at how much you cut off. How much did it end up being?"

"A foot," she said proudly, dropping the Mary Poppins accent. "Donated it all to your mom's foundation."

Faith bent to hug her. Even in the platforms, Violet barely reached her collarbone. "I'm so proud of you."

Violet wagged a finger at her. "You need to tell your mom to send it to a good home."

"She already found one. It'll make a wig for a fierce little girl with leukemia. She's a fighter."

"Good." Her friend surveyed the crowd, nose wrinkled. "Where's jackass? You dump him yet?"

"No…but we had another fight, or something like it, on

the way over." Faith wrapped her arms around her middle. "I need to tell him. I just don't know how. I'm such a chicken."

"You aren't a chicken. You're worried about how he'll react. He usually does the dumping, and his ego's going to take a blow. Just do me a favor and don't stay with him because you feel bad." A crash of metal rang out from the lakeshore, followed by an "oh, shit!" and laughter. "Damn it. I should go see what got destroyed. It better not be Dad's bass boat, or I'm dead."

Violet hurried into the dark, yelling, "What did you do? What. Did. You. *Do?*"

Faith shook her head. Whoever it was needed to run while they had a chance, otherwise, the mad pixie of Suttonville would grind them into glitter and use it to decorate her room. Laughing at the thought, she wandered into the kitchen. Trays of snacks covered every surface, and a game of beer pong had started at the table.

"Where's Cam?" one of the guys at the table asked her. "He should play."

She shrugged. "Not sure. I just came in."

"Didn't he go upstairs?" Skye Jacobs pointed through the kitchen door to the living room. "I thought I saw him."

Probably to drink and pout alone. "Thanks."

If he was up there, maybe this was the right time to tell him it was over. Then she could get back to the party with a clear conscience, and help Vi keep the peace so her house would still be standing by dawn.

"Faith? Um…" Skye twisted a strand of strawberry-blond hair around her finger.

She paused in the doorway. "Yes?"

Skye blanched. "It's…nothing. Never mind."

Frowning, Faith left the kitchen and headed for the stairs. Had Cameron said something to Skye? Had he been an ass to everyone because he was upset? Or was it something else? At this point, anything was possible. Maybe he was changing into a werewolf and didn't want anyone to see. It *was* a full moon tonight, after all.

The living room was empty, but she heard a thump and laughter upstairs. She climbed up slowly, dreading this conversation. How mad would he be? Would he cause a scene, or let her go? Vi was right—he didn't take well to blows against his ego. She'd seen that during football season every time he fumbled a catch.

All the upstairs doors were closed. Faith stood in the dim hallway staring at them. How awkward was this? What if she went into the wrong one? The last thing she needed tonight was walking in on a hookup.

A male voice rumbled behind the guest bedroom door at the end of the hallway. It sounded like Cameron. And it sounded like he wasn't alone. What was he up to?

She strode to the door and wrenched it open, then jumped back so fast, she hit the wall behind her. "You...you..."

Cameron looked blearily up at her. Holly Masterson rushed to drag a sheet over herself. Neither one of them was dressed—not at all—and Holly's blond hair stuck out wildly, like she'd been caught in a wind tunnel.

Anger sparked an inferno in Faith's chest. "Wow, Holly. You might want to redo your hair before you go downstairs. Then again, Cam always overuses his hands. That's why he fumbles whatever he catches."

Cameron's face turned bright red. He dragged a pillow into his lap and sat up. "As if you'd know. We never made it past second base. I got sick of waiting."

Disgusted, she turned to go. "Screw you. Or better yet, screw her. We're done."

She slammed the door behind her and stomped downstairs, managing to make it to the guest bathroom before she burst out laughing and crying at the same time.

Chapter Five

Kyle's alarm went off early. He'd promised Mrs. Gladwell he'd come over around ten, but he had two lawns to mow first. He must be the only dumbass getting up at seven on the first day of spring break.

He shoved back the covers, marveling at the bruise on his right side. Dennings's pitching speed was getting much better, but his control still needed work. That little love tap yesterday left a mark.

After rolling from bed, he staggered through a shower, then dressed in old cargo shorts and a T-shirt. By the time he made it downstairs, Grandpa already had coffee going, and Dad was reading *The Wall Street Journal* — a paper copy.

"Dad, are you ever going to get an electronic subscription? I bought you an iPad for Christmas, remember?" Kyle asked, grabbing a mug from the cabinet. "You're killing trees, buying that thing."

"Electronic newspapers don't read the same." Dad never

looked up from the stock pages. "You off to work?"

"Yep, and I'm seeing a new customer this morning." He snagged a cinnamon oatmeal muffin from the plate Grandpa had set out before heading to the table. "That makes twelve."

"Really?" Dad put his paper down. Pride sparkled in his eyes. "I'm impressed."

"You should go to landscape design school after you graduate," Grandpa said in his craggy voice. "Traditional college isn't for you."

Dad sighed, but Kyle felt a surge of gratitude. The idea of getting a degree in business or finance, or even general studies, sounded so daunting when held up against his dyslexia. Taking the SAT had made him feel like throwing up, and his score wasn't good for anything but laughing at. No, college wasn't for him. Especially when he didn't need a degree. "I like the sound of that."

"But—" Dad started, but Grandpa waved him off.

"Dean, I know you think college is the way to go, but I didn't go to college and I built up a multimillion dollar company with a band saw and some elbow grease. I built this kitchen table, and a thousand more just like it. Let the kid do what he's good at." Grandpa chuckled. "Lord knows he needs an honest living. Those young people who do nothing but party and spend up their parents' money their whole lives irritate the shit out of me."

Kyle laughed, especially when his dad gave Grandpa a sour look. The three of them, around the kitchen table, looked like a past, present, future picture of one man. Dad had inherited Grandpa's dark hair, blue eyes, and height—and Kyle had inherited his Dad's. One now completely gray, one silver-streaked, and one as dark-haired as the crows cawing in the backyard. Despite that, they were pretty different people. Grandpa was an old-fashioned businessman who could sell you a handful of illegally picked bluebonnets. Dad was the finance whiz, investing the money after Grandpa sold the company, making them a fortune his grandkids couldn't outspend.

Some days Kyle wasn't sure where he fit in that picture.

His good mood soured a little. "I better get to work."

"Home by seven? Rosanna left us a King Ranch casserole for dinner."

He waved as he went out the garage door. Their housekeeper always made them food for the weekends, worrying that "her men" would eat Chinese takeout if she didn't provide.

She was probably right.

Ever since Mom and Grandma died, the house had slowly unraveled into a bachelor pad, and Rosanna had her work cut out for her just trying to stem the tide. Kyle had only been three when they'd gotten in the car accident and he didn't remember much about it, taking his life with Dad and Grandpa totally for granted.

Maybe that's why he found it hard to talk to girls—he hadn't been around any at home for a long time.

The pickup had a little trouble starting, but he got it rolling and drove to his first job. Even at 8:00 a.m., a strong, warm breeze blew in from the west, and it was humid enough to make his back sweat in the early morning sun. By the time he finished his second lawn—an acre sea of spring green that needed to be mowed down short to allow the new growth to take hold—he had dirt, dead grass, and flecks of pollen stuck all over his legs and arms. Great, not the best first impression for the Gladwell job.

After brushing himself off as best he could, he drove to their house, the Toyota rattling like a dying animal when he cut the ignition. Mrs. Gladwell was already on the porch. Tall, slim, with a long neck, she looked more like a retired dancer than the president of a charity. She waved at him, smiling, when he got out of the truck.

"This way," she called, heading around the side of the house. "We'll go on back."

He followed her into their backyard, then grunted in sympathy. "You weren't wrong."

"I know." Her voice had an exasperated edge. "The landscaper told us all this....vegetation would create an classic environment. Instead, we got—"

"A jungle. I hate when those companies overdo it. Less is more with a backyard sometimes," Kyle said. "Okay, the first problem is your oak needs pruned, badly. The bald spots in the lawn are where the Bermuda isn't getting enough sun. It's a high-sun grass, and all this shade is killing it."

They walked around the backyard, and he pointed out places where he'd take out half the ornamental bushes, prune others back, and where he'd need to put in some new sod. "Mrs. Gladwell, this is a pretty big job. I can get a good start this weekend, but it's going to be kind of expensive."

"That's fine," she said in a rush. "This luncheon...I have a former governor's wife coming, along with a number of very wealthy donors. I'm willing to spend whatever it takes to fix this."

He shrugged. "Okay, then. How about I get started on pulling out some of these bushes today and tomorrow, then Monday I can go to the nursery and pick up whatever else we need."

"You're a lifesaver, Kyle." She gave his shoulder a quick pat. "If you need to come in and get a drink of water or use the facilities, feel free."

He nodded, knowing full well he'd never track his dirt all over their house. There was a gas station a block away if he needed anything. "All I need is some extra trash bags."

Once she dashed off, he looked around the backyard again, feeling equal parts excited and apprehensive. This would be the biggest job he'd ever done, and a governor's wife would see it. It had to be perfect.

Nodding to himself, he pulled on his work gloves and went to grab a shovel and his hedge clippers.

Chapter Six

Faith

"One, two, three…one, two three," Faith sang to her little charges. "Second position, backs straight. One, two, three."

Hannah, the world's cutest six-year-old, smiled and showed off the gap where her two front teeth should be. "Miss Faith? Can we do hip-hop now?"

Faith almost laughed at the innocent tone in Hannah's voice, and barely kept it in. "Just a few more minutes of ballet first, okay? One, two, three. One, two, three."

The little ones paid attention for another sixty seconds before wiggling like crazy, so Faith relented and put on "I Like to Move It." Squeals of delight went around the studio and the first graders hurried into place to start their hip-hop routine. Through the observation window, Faith saw the parents whip out cameras to snap pictures of their little darlings. She wished they loved ballet as much as she did, but this was the fun part for all of them.

"Okay! Crisscross. Clap, clap, clap!"

Once class was over, Faith went to the barre and did some stretches. She had an hour before the next class came in, and Madame Schuler let her use the studio to practice after she was done teaching for the day. Lifting her leg onto the barre, she bent her body from side to side, arm up and curved over her head. Her back loosened up and her calves stretched in a satisfying way. For the first time since catching Cameron last night, she felt a little less wound up.

She breathed deep and slow, letting her body settle itself. Why couldn't it be this easy to relax her mind? Even though she'd planned to break it off with him, it hurt to know he'd throw her away without so much as a word. That didn't matter, though. She was free for the first time in months. She should focus on that. She could do what she wanted *when* she wanted, even if that was to come up to the studio and dance until her toes ached.

Warmed up, she went to her dance bag to pull on her pointe shoes and put on some classical music. When she grabbed her phone, though, a long, *long* string of texts from Violet showed on the home screen.

V: *Are you okay?*

That one was from last night. She'd left the party after calling her mom to pick her up. Mom hadn't made a big deal out of it, thankfully, but had seemed happy to know Cameron was out of the picture. Once Faith was home, she'd shoved her phone into her bag and gone straight to bed for a good cry and a long sleep.

Now, though, she realized she should've checked in, because the next few messages were alarming.

V: *That bastard! Do you even…*

V: *He's telling everyone he dumped you. Shit on a*

shingle! I'm going to kill him.

That was bad enough, but an hour later, it got even worse.

V: *Girl, he just told five football assholes that he dumped you because, and I quote, "She was a coldhearted bitch. Couldn't warm her up to save my life."*

V: *I kicked his ass out after that, but...oh God, girl, the damage is done. Everyone is talking about it. Hell, Holly's bragging that she's "no little girl" like you. I kicked her out, too.*

Faith sucked in a breath. Cameron was telling everyone he dumped her...because she hadn't slept with him? A hand flew to cover her mouth and her stomach churned around the granola bar she'd eaten for breakfast. He was telling the whole school she was a bitch?

That *asshole.*

She dialed Violet's number, then savagely tied on her pointe shoes while it rang.

"Hello? Faith?" Violet sounded worried.

"Tell me this is a nightmare. That he's not going around trashing me."

"I can't," Vi said. "I want to wring his neck, but I can't because my hands are too little and his neck is too thick, the bastard."

Faith growled in frustration and stood. She wanted to whirl around this room like a dervish, then drive to Cameron's house and kick him in the balls. "First he cheats on me, then he decides to tell his friends I'm a bitch?"

"Yeah. I don't know what to say, girl." Violet cackled. "Except to get revenge."

"Well, obviously, but how?"

"Sleep with the first guy you see."

She made an impatient noise. "Not possible since that'll be the janitor at the studio. Besides, I'm waiting on Mr. Right."

"There's no such thing, but you be you." Violet chuckled darkly. "You need to make a statement, though. It doesn't matter if you're still a virgin as long as no one believes it. Make them think—rightly—that *he* was the problem."

Was that even possible? Faith raised herself up en pointe, considering. A thousand girls in black leotards and pink tights wearing her face stared back at her in the mirrors covering the studio walls, each one uncertain, all angry. Would anyone believe it if she did what Vi said? Could she act that well?

She'd just landed the lead in the school play. Of course she could.

"You're right. I need to do something."

After they ended their call, she punched up some Tchaikovsky on her phone and did pirouettes until her head was dizzy. It was the only way to drown out the rage—and humiliation. She had to find a way to get back at that bastard. But how?

The hour passed before she came to an answer, and she hurried to pack up her gear and pull shorts over her leotard as the noon tap class started to filter into the studio. Whatever she was going to do, it had to be big.

By the time she made it home, took a smoothie from Mom's outstretched hand, and went upstairs to shower, six Snapchat notifications, all from different people, had popped up on her phone:

A sad-faced Skye: *I'm so sorry about last night. I should've warned you. I feel awful.*

An angry Piper: *I'm at the mall and there's some asinine shit coming out of Cameron's mouth right now. Should I punch him?*

A gossipy Fiona: *Is it true that Cameron dumped you?*

A sneering Mitchell: *You as cold as Cam says?*

A dumbfounded Katrina: *Holly is telling everyone at the mall that she stole Cam from you because you don't put out. Want me to dump a Slurpee in her hair?*

A smirking Jackson: *My car overheated. I heard you could cool it down for me. How about it, ice queen?*

Tears of rage filled Faith's eyes, especially when a new Snapchat chimed: Cameron, sending her a picture of Holly sitting in his lap at the party last night. The message read: *Trading up.*

She squeezed her phone in her hand. What was she going to do? She had half a mind to tell Kat to pour that Slurpee down Holly's shirt and Piper to punch Cam in the throat. But that wouldn't solve anything. Not at all.

No, she needed something bigger. Faith wandered to her window to stare outside and organize her thoughts. Except when she caught sight of the ripped, shirtless guy in her backyard, she forgot what she'd been thinking about.

"Who's *that?*" she whispered, touching the glass.

His back and shoulders flexed under tanned skin. A black tattoo—was it a bird?—was on one of his shoulder blades. There was a bruise on his side, too, but she couldn't make herself wonder about it. The guy's dark hair was in his face as he tugged hard at a holly bush, yanking it from the ground.

Look at those arms. Faith stared, her mouth open. Who was he?

The holly bush gave way and he tipped back, dirt flying. Faint laughter drifted up through her window as he climbed to his feet with his prize, and she caught a look at his face.

She gasped. Holy crap, that was Kyle Sawyer. The stories she'd heard about him were numerous, and if a quarter were true, he was *not* the kind of guy she'd want to talk to. He shoplifted, vandalized buildings, drank, hung out with college students—*girls.* College *girls.* And rumor had it he ran illegal street races with his Charger.

So why did he look like he was having a blast ransacking her backyard? He had an awfully nice smile for such a bad boy.

A thought exploded in her brain—wait a minute...*bad boy*. Kyle was the one guy at Suttonville High who'd seen enough action to have his own lore. His exploits were darker than sin, and being with him was an instant reputation-killer for any girl at Suttonville.

This was it. *Kyle* would be her revenge.

Chapter Seven

KYLE

That holly tree hadn't wanted to leave the ground, but he conquered it. Sure, it had gone down fighting, scratching his arm with one of its barbed leaves, and he still won. Grinning at the mess—his chest was speckled with dirt, and he probably had some in his hair, too—he broke down the branches and tossed it into his mulch pile.

He wiped a hand across his forehead and went to gulp down water from the thermos he brought from home. It was after noon from the position of the sun, and his stomach growled. He needed to clean up a little and go grab some lunch. He'd made a good start, though.

The back door banged shut and he turned, expecting Mrs. Gladwell to be checking on his progress. Instead, a tall, slender girl with huge brown eyes and brown hair up in a bun walked his way.

No, she didn't walk. She glided. A dancer—her movements would've told him that, even if she hadn't been wearing a black leotard with shorts pulled over it. And she was headed straight for him. Hurriedly, he brushed the dirt off his chest. It smeared with his sweat, leaving streaks of mud across his pecs. Great. Just awesome. Now he couldn't even put on his shirt to cover it up without using a hose.

"You're Kyle Sawyer," she said, no trace of doubt in her voice.

Based on her wary expression, his reputation preceded him. "Yep. And you are?"

"Faith. Faith Gladwell."

She frowned, but she couldn't hide the quick glance at his chest. Was it the dirt that had her attention? Or was it him? He bit back a smile. Maybe he didn't need the shirt after all.

She blushed when she noticed him watching her and pointedly looked around at the holes dotting the ground. "Why are you tearing up my backyard?"

"Your mom asked me to," he said. Yeah, because that wasn't a stupid answer. Dumbass. "I'm fixing it up for her."

Faith walked over to peer at the pile of branches and dug-up plants. "Really? Because it looks like an F2 tornado went through here."

He shrugged. "Sometimes you have to make a mess to fix one."

"You're telling me," she muttered.

"What?"

She shook herself. "Nothing."

But it wasn't nothing—he could tell by the way her jaw was clenched. This girl was on the verge of tears. He knew pain when he saw it. "Something wrong? Or are you worried I might be vandalizing your yard?"

She laughed, then looked stunned by it. "You're funny."

He couldn't help smiling. It wasn't often a girl told him that. "I try. You okay?"

"Not really." She bit her lip, and he found it mesmerizing.

Faith was a pretty girl, he had to admit. She caught him looking, and a little smirk twitched at the corner of her mouth. "Actually, I came out here to ask you for a favor."

"Me?"

"Yeah, you." She sat down on the patio steps and motioned for him to sit next to her. "I have a problem, and you might be the solution."

He took a seat, curious, but careful to keep his expression neutral. He didn't need her thinking he was interested. That wasn't his style, or so he let everyone believe. "I'm listening."

"This is kind of weird…just hear me out, 'kay?"

"I like weird."

Faith laughed. "Yeah, I guessed that already. Anyway, my boyfriend and I broke up last night. Now he's telling everyone he dumped me because I'm…" She blinked fast, and her face flushed. "Because I'm a coldhearted bitch. Or so he says, because I wouldn't sleep with him. The truth is I caught him in bed with Holly Masterson."

"God, his taste is pathetic if he went after that girl." Kyle shook his head. Holly always looked at him like he was gum on her shoe, and in every class they'd shared, she had a tendency to play dumb, which he didn't find cute whatsoever. "She's not the nicest person in the world."

"You can say that again." Faith swallowed hard. "I need to make this right, though. The rumor is out, big-time. I'm hearing it from everyone."

"That sucks, but why do you care what they think?" he asked. "Sounds to me like you dodged a bullet if your dick ex is talking trash about you like that. By the way—who's the boyfriend?"

"Cameron Zimmerman."

Kyle leaned away from her, unable to keep from reacting no matter how much he wanted to look unaffected. Cameron? She *dated* that d-bag? He and his idiot football buddies were the main reason Kyle had turned himself into the scariest guy at Suttonville. If a guy thought you might pull a switchblade on him, he stopped trying to shove you inside a locker. Bulking up and making the baseball team had helped, too, but still…

"Damn."

"So you know him." Faith's voice was flat.

"Um…yeah."

"Then maybe my favor will make a little sense." She took a deep breath and smoothed a few hairs back into the tight bun she wore. "See, I need to prove him wrong, but telling people won't work. I have football players already texting and Snapchatting me the most vile things. I need to put him in his place in a way that will shut them all up. I need *proof* he's wrong about me."

Kyle couldn't stop the smile spreading across his face. Helping this girl get revenge on Cameron couldn't be a bad thing, no matter what she suggested. He had an ax to grind with that prick himself, and Faith seemed like a good way to do it. "Tell me about this plan of yours."

Chapter Eight

FAITH

She couldn't believe it—he was *smiling* at her. She didn't think Kyle ever smiled—not that she'd heard of, anyway. It seemed like she wasn't the only one with a beef against Cameron. How lucky could she get? She'd thought he'd laugh at her, brush her off as one of those popular girls not worth his time.

But she wasn't that popular, and he definitely seemed to have time for a little revenge.

Hope—an angry, hard, shining thing—crashed around her chest. "Okay, so you have a…a…"

"Reputation?" Kyle said, his smile going to full-on grin. It was a little scary. "Like maybe I steal walkers from old ladies at the supermarket and use them to break church windows?"

Faith laughed—she couldn't help it. She also couldn't help staring at those blue, blue eyes of his. Goodness. "Yeah, something like that. But it's more that I've heard you've been with lots of girls. Older girls, mostly."

His grin faded. "Yeah, so?"

"Well, what if everyone thought we were hooking up? You and me?" God, he was going to start laughing at her any second. She was in too deep to stop now, though. "Everyone would totally know Cameron's wrong. About me being frosty, if you know what I mean. If I'm dating a notorious bad boy, then they'll think I'm having the hottest sex of my life and that I don't give a damn about Cameron."

"And why would they think you're having the hottest sex of your life?" He sounded hesitant and amused. Not the best combination, but at least he wasn't blowing her off.

"Because you'll say so. You'll drop that information into circulation and let it run its course."

"So, you want me to pretend to be your boyfriend," he said, scratching his head. "And start a rumor that we're having scorching sex as often as possible?"

"Yes," she said. "I know it's a weird request, but he's out telling everyone that I'm…I'm…"

"A sexual glacier. You've said that already," Kyle said. "Are you? Or was it just Cameron?"

"No! I mean, yes. I mean…Jesus, why would you ask me that?"

His eyes were shining, totally teasing her. "It seems relevant."

Oh God. No wonder he had college girls all over him—that playful little smirk would work on a nun. This was such a bad idea, but his smile made her brain misfire, so her mouth went on without its assistance. "I just…I don't want to be with someone unless I love them, you know?"

Oh, why did I tell him that? Why? He's going to die laughing.

But he didn't. Instead, he shrugged, stowing the player and morphing back into the standoffish bad boy. "And you don't love Cameron?"

What was with this guy and his questions? "I thought I

did," she said. "But I didn't. And he didn't love me. I don't think he even cared about me that much."

Kyle was quiet a moment, another one of those little smirks tugging at the corner of his mouth. She couldn't get a good read on him, but a bead of sweat ran down his chest and she had to force her eyes to meet his. Even under all that dirt, he was hotter than a July afternoon. Was this a good idea? Kyle was dangerous. He was trouble.

Except… She studied him. Kyle looked anything but trouble right now, in dirty shorts with a stripe of mud across his forehead. He looked normal, like someone she could trust. Maybe even…nice.

And why the hell couldn't she keep her eyes on his face? Who cared if he was built like the statue of David? Then her eyes drifted to his arms. He played baseball, she remembered, and worked outside. From those muscles, she bet he could carry her and a load of firewood at the same time. Cameron had been more stringy—a running back, lean and quick. Kyle was lean, but packed with muscle. What would it be like to run a hand over those biceps?

Damn it. Focus.

Finally, he said, "Cameron and his friends treated me like shit in middle school, and he still treats some friends of mine that way. But I especially don't like assholes who treat girls badly. For all my…faults, I like girls." His smirk turned into a secretive smile. "Guys like Cameron should get hit on the nose every once in a while, just for existing and making people miserable."

She let out the breath she was holding. "Does that mean you'll do it?"

"Sure, why not?" he said. "I don't know why you'd pick me for this experiment, but I'm not seeing anyone right now, so I'm in. Anything to make Cameron look like an idiot."

Faith couldn't believe it. Could. Not. Believe. It. He was

really going to do this. "Thank you! So…if we're really going to do this, we'll need to be seen together some. Both at school and other places. Is that okay?"

"Fine by me." He looked around her backyard. "And I'm going to be over here a lot, working. If you invite me inside when your parents aren't here, and you have nosy neighbors, that could get stories started." He paused. "Are you sure you really want to do this? I mean, no big deal to me, but are you sure you want to, uh, tarnish your reputation by hanging out with me?"

Determination welled up inside her. "Yes. As long as my parents don't get sucked in—they're pretty protective—I'm totally fine with this."

"Okay, then." He blew out a breath. "I better get back to work. We can talk more tomorrow."

She had to force herself to be still and not dance around the yard in triumph. "Tomorrow it is. And Kyle? Thank you. This is going to be the best trick ever pulled at Suttonville High."

As she drifted inside, she thought she heard him say, "If you say so, princess."

Chapter Nine

KYLE

After Faith went back inside — wearing this smile that would make an ax murderer run — Kyle started cleaning out the brush in the backyard, all thoughts of lunch forgotten. In fact, it kind of felt like a train wreck was in progress in his stomach. He'd tried to play it cool, to act like he was only kind of interested, no strings attached, but his rage against Cameron had almost gotten the better of him. The real problem, though, was Faith. How close would he have to let her get?

How far would he have to go to keep up the story? Would they have to be caught making out to spread the rumors faster?

Sweat beaded on his forehead, and it had nothing to do with the midafternoon heat. God, what had he gotten himself into? Was he really going to risk his peace at school by taking on Cameron and his friends? He'd finally found a comfortable place, free of those bastards, and now he was hitting them head-on by "seducing" Cameron's ex.

Just chill. It wasn't like he actually had to sleep with her. Convincing people wouldn't be hard, even without much evidence. Tell a few guys on the team when they had practice that he'd hooked up with Faith during the break, and it would be out. He wouldn't have to do anything much to keep it going.

But still.

It was one thing to create a persona for himself—if things went wrong it was his own damn fault. Faith, though? He didn't know her well enough to tell what she was really like, but she seemed like one of those nice girls who would move to the other side of the hall if he headed her way. A shiny dancer girl with a clean image. It seemed a shame that she'd throw all that away on a little revenge, but guys like Cameron brought the worst out in people for damn sure.

Kyle tidied up the pile of broken branches, then went for a spade and a crowbar. He needed to work off his anxiety, and there were a few large photinias along the fence that needed to go. Why the hell did anyone plant these? They took over yards, spread fungus, and they weren't all that much to look at. They also were a pain to dig out, and that's exactly what he needed right now. Hard labor and a vendetta. Well, that, and time to imagine the look on Cameron's face when he heard the news.

He hacked at those photinias like they'd done him personal harm. Just thinking about that asshole made some horrible memories surface. His first run-in with Cameron's pack at school had been in seventh grade. The memory still stung.

They'd swaggered into the bathroom, following him inside. Then, they'd all been bigger than him.

"Who's the shrimp?" Cameron had asked, voice cracking on the last word.

Kyle, stupidly, had glared at him. "Why do you sound like

a girl?"

That one comment. That one jab—it had started everything. Two of Cameron's friends had grabbed him and forced him to his knees in front of the toilet. He'd never forget Cameron's sneer as he forced Kyle's head into the bowl and flushed.

They'd left, laughing their asses off. Kyle was too ashamed to leave, and hid in the bathroom for the last two periods before calling Grandpa for a ride. He'd cried, trying to keep Grandpa from seeing, but he'd noticed.

"Kid, one of these days," he'd said, his voice deep and commanding, "you'll have a chance to knock them off their high horses. When it comes, do it, and don't look back."

With Faith's offer, it looked his best chance had come. He just needed to take it. Still, the memory left a bitter taste in his mouth. To this day, he hated himself for not fighting sooner, harder.

Kyle slammed the spade into the ground, ripping up the roots of the hedge. The only way to forget would be to work so hard his hands blistered and his brain went dark. And that's exactly what he did. He disappeared into a world of green, of aching muscles, of earth. And he didn't want to come back.

Sometime later, hours by the slant of the sun, Mrs. Gladwell called, "Kyle?"

He jumped, dropping the spade, and pulled his earbuds out of his ears. Judging by her amused smile, she'd been calling to him for a while. "Um, sorry. Yes?"

"Honey, it's almost six. You've been at this a while. Maybe you should take a break and come back tomorrow?"

Almost *six*? He looked down and winced. His legs, arms, and chest were caked with dirt and he had a half dozen new scratches. It looked like he'd been mud wrestling a tiger. And the backyard was a disaster.

"Oh, um, I should clean up everything first."

Mrs. Gladwell chuckled. She had a nice laugh—kind, not mocking. A total mom-amused-by-a-kid laugh. "As long as you promise to come back tomorrow, I think we can leave it. I must say, I'm impressed by the level of, uh, *destruction*."

He flushed. At least she wasn't pissed about all the holes, mounds of dirt, and stacks of branches. "Don't worry—it'll look brand-new by the time I finish with it."

"I trust you." She handed him his T-shirt. "Now run along home. I'm sure your folks are wondering where you are."

"Yes, ma'am," he said meekly, his cheeks going hot. *I'm such an idiot.* "I'll be back by eight tomorrow, if that's okay. I'll let myself into the backyard."

"That sounds great. Thanks, Kyle."

As soon as she went back inside, he pulled the shirt over his head and collected all his tools, marveling at the mess he'd made. He'd lost all track of time, going into a zone he normally reserved for games, but instead thinking about his deal with Faith.

Apprehension prickled down his back. A sure sign that he might've made a mistake saying yes. How long could he make her—and everyone else—believe he wasn't a complete dork around girls? He wanted to pull this off, to show up Cameron, but it could blow up in *his* face instead.

Suddenly, he felt like he was being watched, and he glanced up at the second-story windows. The blinds on the right-hand window shifted against the glass.

Had Faith been watching him all this time? Huh.

He stared up at the window, waiting. A minute passed, then the blinds fluttered. He smirked when Faith noticed he saw her. Her eyes popped open wide, and the blinds crashed back into place. Feeling a little better about everything, he went to the Toyota.

Who knew—this might be fun after all.

"Kyle? That you?" Grandpa yelled from the kitchen. The spicy scent of King Ranch casserole hung in the air.

His stomach growled loud enough to answer before he made it out of the mudroom. "Yeah. I'm beat, but dinner smells good."

"You also have enough dirt on your hands to plant petunias. Go clean up," Grandpa said, shaking his head. He wore a red apron over his jeans and Rangers T-shirt, like he actually prepared the meal, even though all he'd done was put dinner in the over to warm up.

"I'm going, I'm going." He yawned his way toward the stairs. "Dad home?"

"In his office. It's tax season."

"Oh, right." Although Dad would be working on Saturday even if it wasn't. Managing his—and other people's—money took a lot of effort. Kyle figured he'd stick to planting trees and mowing lawns. "Be down in a sec."

A shower sounded great, until he actually stood under the hot water. Every scrape and blister he'd earned in Faith's backyard stung at once, making him hiss with pain. He needed to keep his shirt on tomorrow. How would Faith like it if he covered up the scenery, though? He laughed, the sound echoing off the hard walls of the shower. In the course of one afternoon, he'd turned into Faith's boy toy. In more ways than one.

And funny how he kept calling it "Faith's backyard" when she wasn't the one paying him for the job.

After drying off and putting on clean shorts and a T-shirt, he went downstairs to help Grandpa set the table.

"You're awful cheerful for a kid who looks like he got into a fight with a Weed Eater," Grandpa said, giving the scratches on his legs a look. "I guess you won the fight, then?"

Kyle bit back a grin. "Yeah, except I was doing battle with a holly bush."

"Who's the client?"

"You know those commercials for the Gladwell Foundation?"

Grandpa scratched the side of his head with a potholder. "The pretty lady asking for donations to help with juvenile cancer? I think I wrote them a big check last year."

"So did Dad. Mrs. Gladwell is the one who hired me," he said. "She wants me to redo her backyard. It was a freaking mess. Some hotshot landscaper overdid it, and I have to rip out a ton of worthless crap before I can fix it. All their photinias had fungus, and I saw some on the hollies. So they had to go before they ruined the good stuff."

Dad came breezing into the kitchen and went to the fridge. He emerged with two Shiners and flipped one to Grandpa. "Kid, you need to wear jeans and long sleeves if you're going to be diving into someone's flower garden."

Grandpa snorted into his beer. "I think he should wear a lot less than that if he's diving into someone's 'flower garden.'" He made air quotes. "Otherwise, I don't think it'll work out so well."

"Jesus, Dad." Kyle's dad laughed, shaking his head. "Does everything have to go there with you?"

"I may be old, but my plumbing still works. Maven seems to agree." Grandpa nudged Kyle in the side. "How about it, kid? You got yourself a girlfriend?"

Kyle flushed and went to the counter to cut up some bread to go with dinner so he wouldn't have to look at their hopeful faces. "Not exactly, but kind of."

"Kind of?" Dad said.

"Not exactly?" Grandpa said.

"She's a…a friend from school. But I think she likes me." There, maybe that would shut them up. "Actually, she's Mrs. Gladwell's daughter. I, uh, I caught her checking me out while I was working in the backyard." Forcing a little bravado into his voice, he added, "I sort of forgot to put my shirt on for that part."

Grandpa roared with laughter, and Dad pinched the bridge of his nose between two fingers, but he looked pleased. Not seeing him with any girls had worried them, and he couldn't exactly tell them what he told guys at school—that he hooked up with college girls on the weekends. Well, he could probably tell *Grandpa* that, and get an "atta boy!" But Dad would give him a twenty-minute lecture on STDs. Hell to the no on that. He wasn't going to endure a lecture for something that wasn't true.

"She pretty?" Dad asked. "This Gladwell girl?"

Relieved he could be honest, he nodded. "A dancer. Great legs. She seems nice, too."

"Good boy," Grandpa said. The oven timer dinged, and he raced to pull the casserole out before it burned up. "Hardworking kid like you? You deserve a sweet, pretty girl on your arm. Bring her by if things get rolling. I'd like to meet her."

"Me, too," Dad said as they sat down to eat.

"Okay," Kyle said weakly, wondering if he could convince Faith to pretend to be his girlfriend for their sake. He made sure to keep his mouth full for most of the meal so he wouldn't have to say anything else.

Chapter Ten

Faith picked at her dinner, still burning with the humiliation of being caught ogling Kyle while he worked. God, he probably thought she was the most stupid girl he'd met. There were days when she thought he might be right. And today had been a real winner.

But those *arms*. Who wouldn't stare at a guy like that attacking greenery with a spade like a knight with a sword? Good gracious…Kyle's biceps alone were living proof there was a God, and that She loved the world.

A chuckle rose in Faith's chest, making her choke on her lasagna. Dad pushed her water glass toward her, while Mom stared anxiously to make sure she was still breathing. She waved them both off. "I'm okay."

"You scared me," Mom said. "Ever since you choked on that grape—"

"I was seven." Faith smiled fondly at her. "You can recover now."

"You know Mom—she'll never waste a chance to fret over her babies." Winking, Dad rose and took his plate to the sink. He paused, peering out the window. "What on earth happened in the yard?"

"Oh! I hired a young man to fix it for us. For the luncheon," Mom answered. "He's a hard worker."

"I'll say," Faith murmured.

Mom shot her an amused look. "I know it looks bad now, but I have a good feeling about this kid. He really seems to know what he's doing. I had to *make* him go home, otherwise I'd bet he'd still be out there working."

"You know him, Faith?" Dad asked.

"Not well," she said, not wanting to spoil Kyle's job by telling her parents about his reputation as Suttonville's resident bad boy. "I didn't even know he did lawn work until today."

"Uh-huh," Mom said, smiling down at her plate. "But you certainly know now."

Dad turned to stare at them. "What do you mean?"

"Oh, nothing." Mom carried her plate to the sink and kissed Dad on the cheek. "Just that he proved his green thumb today."

As they headed out of the kitchen, Faith heard Dad ask, "But how do you know? All I can tell is that he's really good with a shovel."

"I think he'll surprise us," Mom said, her voice fading as they went deeper into the house.

No doubt about that. Was the kitchen warm, or was it just her? With a sigh, Faith washed the dishes, then hurried upstairs. She wanted to text Vi, but hadn't been brave enough to look at her phone. When she did, she almost choked for real.

Sixty-two notifications.

Hands shaking, she opened Snapchat. There were forty-two from guys on the football and track teams, all of them more vile than the next, and some even included pictures a ten-gallon jug of brain bleach couldn't erase. Angrily, she started unfriending every guy Cameron might call "friend." It wouldn't stop them, but she wanted them gone for however long it worked.

Twenty of the other messages, mostly texts, were from girls asking if it was true, letting her know they'd seen Cameron with Holly, or expressing sympathy—some of it fake, some of it real. It was enough to make her want to hurl her phone across the room.

Instead, she called Violet.

"Hey," Vi said. "You okay?"

"No." Faith gulped down air to keep from crying. "That utter, complete douche nozzle."

"Girl, don't put down douche nozzles like that. Call him what he is—a rancid piece of shit."

Faith managed a laugh. "I love you."

"I know." Violet sighed. "Any thoughts on how you're going to play this?"

"No, not thoughts. *Action*," she said, determination welling up in her chest. "I worked out a deal with Kyle Sawyer today."

"*Kyle Sawyer*, the man-whore bad boy? Skateboarder, street racer, troublemaker…*that* Kyle Sawyer?" Violet sounded utterly shocked. "Where in the world did you find him?"

"My backyard." Faith told her all about her encounter. "Vi, he's hotter than the sun and has a rep darker than the devil's. This is going to drive Cameron in-freaking-sane."

"No doubt, but…are you sure?"

"Yes, absolutely. He was nicer than I expected, and has his own problem with Cameron. It's the perfect arrangement."

Violet burst out laughing. "Hell, yes, it is! Okay, here's

what we need to do—because a story isn't going to cut it. You need to talk him into taking you to Dolly's one night this week. The two of you, sitting on the hood of that badass Charger, sharing a shake and whispering in each other's ears? That will light up the rumor mill like nothing else in the world."

Faith picked at her fingernails. This wasn't a mistake, was it? "I'm not sure a drive-in is a place he'd consider going. Too…high school."

"Maybe, but everyone's going to be hanging out there for ice cream this week. Tell him it's a good place to start a rumor and I bet he says yes."

She was right about that. Dolly's was *the* hangout when there wasn't a party going on. Kyle might think it was lame, but Violet had a point. "I'll ask him tomorrow."

"Ooh, can I come over? I want to inspect the merchandise."

Faith laughed. "Why not? He already knows I'm spying on him."

"I want to meet him, make sure he's not a freak," Violet said. "Getting a gander would be a plus, though."

Doubt sank into her bones and she flopped back on her bed, arm flung over her eyes. "Do you think I'm doing the right thing?"

"What was that text from Michael?" Violet's voice was hard.

Frustration filled Faith's chest again, a hard, burning kernel. She needed to grab her courage with both hands and see this through. "Good point. Okay, rabid affair with a bad boy it is. See you tomorrow?"

"Yep, I'll be there around noon."

"Better make it one—I have church."

"Oh, of course. Your parents would never let you forget that."

Faith stared up at her ceiling, wondering if God was watching. "It's not too bad. I kind of like going."

"Better you than me," Violet said. "I'd go up like dry kindling if I crossed the threshold."

"That's because your life is more interesting than mine."

"Heh, not for much longer."

Laughing, they ended the call and Faith turned on the "do not disturb" feature on her phone to stop the notifications for the night. She wrapped a quilt around her shoulders and sat up to stare out the window. The little bit of light from the back porch glowed across the yard, highlighting the holes in the ground. Kyle had thoroughly destroyed the backyard. Would he destroy her reputation that thoroughly, too? And if he did, was it going to make things better or worse?

Faith rolled her ankles, stretching out the tendons and muscles. She'd looked forward to graduation and NYU for so long, but had wanted to enjoy senior year. Now, though, she'd give anything for it to be over, and that sucked.

She sat up straighter, glaring at her reflection in the window, strands from her bun falling in wisps around her face. Maybe working with Kyle was a mistake, but no matter what happened, she was going to make Cameron wish he'd never opened his mouth.

Sunlight streamed through her window, and Faith groaned. She'd been having a weird dream about a giant pair of tap shoes chasing her around the studio, but it hadn't been bad enough to wake her up. What time was it? She dug her phone out from under her pillow. Eight thirty? They didn't have to leave for church for two hours. Why the heck was she awake?

A motor rumbled to life outside. Groggy, Faith stumbled over her dance bag on the way to the window. Kyle, holding what looked like a chain saw and wearing safety glasses, was attacking the pile of branches in the corner of her backyard.

Mesmerized, she watched him wield the saw, his forearms taut and straining.

"Faith?" Mom called from downstairs. "You awake? Dad wants to leave early and grab doughnuts on the way to church."

Um, yeah. Church—not drooling over boys with chain saws. "Okay!"

Footsteps sounded on the stairs, and Faith raced back to her bed, landing just before Mom opened the door. "Did the noise wake you?"

"It did, but I needed to get up and do my stretches anyway. I've got a lot of dancing ahead of me with the musical."

A little smile twitched at the corner of Mom's mouth. "Don't you usually do those on the back porch?"

Their back porch, screened in with a smooth painted hardwood floor, was the closest thing to a studio in the house. Blushing, she looked down at her quilt. "Yes. Do you think I'll be in his way?"

"Oh, probably not." Chuckling, Mom turned to go. "But do the poor boy a favor. Wait until he puts away the saw. I don't want to be responsible for any lost limbs."

Faith rolled her eyes as soon as her mother closed the door. Was she that obvious? No…she couldn't be. Still, blushing every time Mom asked about Kyle was probably a dead giveaway that she had a little crush.

And that's all it will be, right? Sighing, she pulled a clean leotard, tights, and shorts out of dresser. That's all it *had* to be. They were in the business of revenge. Nothing else.

Chapter Eleven

The morning air was a little brisk today, and the dew was taking its own sweet time burning off the grass. Kyle turned off the saw and took a deep breath, letting the cool air clear his lungs of the dust. So far, no one had come outside to yell at him for running equipment this early, but most of the homeowners had lawn crews, and were probably used to the sweet sounds of mowers at 8:00 a.m.

He wiped his forehead and gathered a load of branches to take to the truck. At this rate, he'd have to run to Mark's Nursery by lunchtime. They paid for wood to make mulch — either in cash or product, and he'd need a lot of mulch to fix up the Gladwells' flower beds. Maybe he'd break even with all this stuff.

On his way back, he happened to glance into the screened-in back porch and stopped dead in his tracks.

Faith had one leg up on a rail built into the back wall and was stretching toward it with her arm over her head.

She was wearing another one of those leotards, along with pink tights and a pair of ballet shoes. Classical music wafted out into the yard, and she moved with it, graceful and sure. However emotional and uncertain she'd been yesterday, here she was all confidence. Her leg, toes pointed, was flexed, and he marveled at the muscles she'd built up. He hadn't seen a pair of calves that perfect…well, ever. The rest of her was as long and lean. Her arms moved slow and smooth, like they were cutting through water, and her long neck arched as she turned her body.

Kyle's breath hitched. He'd never seen anything quite so beautiful. If she looked like this just stretching, what did she look like when she danced?

He had to see that. He *had* to.

She bent forward, touching her raised leg, then straightened up. And caught him gawking. For a second she stared back—then a slow smirk crossed her face. *Uh-huh, payback's a bitch*, he could hear her thinking.

Before he could stop himself, he said, "You're pretty flexible."

The smirk turned a little wicked. "You have no idea."

His whole body flushed, but he jerked his chin at her, cocky. "Is this part of the game, or are you offering to prove it?"

Faith lowered her leg, looking flustered. "Um…"

"Faith?" her mom called from inside. "Time to get ready for church!"

Kyle sighed inwardly. *My big fat mouth. Jesus.* "Part of the game, then. Okay, I'm up for playing. I'm afraid it's going to be pretty warm this afternoon. I might just have to work without my shirt on."

"You're a mess," she said, but she smiled, and it lit him up inside. It was such a *real* smile—nothing behind it but happiness and a little mischief. "But if that's your offer, I'll have to find that telescope my uncle got me for Christmas in seventh grade."

He took a step closer to the screen window. "Or you could come sit out here, drink an iced tea, watch the show."

She looked at him through lowered eyelashes. "I do enjoy a nice glass of sweet tea."

This girl was going to send him into orbit. She flirted like a pro—how did she end up with Cameron? He was an empty skull in football pads. "Shade's nice out here, too."

Faith paused, about to say something, but her mother called, "Faith! We're leaving in thirty minutes. Let Kyle get back to work and go change!"

Faith jumped, looking guilty. "Coming!" She gave him a quick nod. "I'll see you this afternoon. Keep that brashness going—you're going to meet my best friend and she's not for the faint of heart."

"Looking forward to it," he said, surprised she was willing to introduce him to people. Then again, the friend probably knew the deal. "Have fun at church."

"I will." And it sounded like she meant it. "See you later."

She went inside, leaving him feeling like he'd taken a right hook to the jaw. Faith wasn't exactly what he expected. And that could be dangerous.

Wonderful, but dangerous.

After running to the nursery to drop off the branches he'd cut up—and to barter for a bunch of mulch—Kyle sat in his truck eating a hamburger. The backyard looked less like a disaster area. There was still some demo work to do, but he'd be able to start planting tomorrow.

The Gladwells' car pulled past him into the driveway. He hopped out of his truck as Mrs. Gladwell, wearing a rose-colored dress complete with a string of pearls and a matching purse, came walking over. Faith flashed him a little smile over her mother's shoulder. She'd changed into a pale blue sundress and a white sweater. Definitely church wear, but she made it look good. Shaking her head at his staring, she chuckled and disappeared into the house.

"So, how's it going?" Mrs. Gladwell asked.

"Good. I'll be ready to shop for plants tomorrow. Anything you'd like?"

"I trust you." She turned toward a man in suit. He had Faith's eyes, but where she was tall and lean like her mother, he was stocky and compact. "Kyle, this is my husband."

"Mr. Gladwell." He held out a hand to shake, realizing too late he had a streak of mustard from his hamburger on his palm. He pulled it back quickly. "Sorry. I'm kind of a mess."

"No worries. Any high schooler who can handle a chain saw like you is okay in my book." He smiled. "Not a lot of guys your age are willing to work like that."

Kyle shrugged, embarrassed. "I enjoy it. Um…" Ugh, he hated this part. "I'll need to know your budget, so I don't go too crazy with the plants."

"It's entirely up to you." Mrs. Gladwell smiled. "Like I said, I trust you."

Mr. Gladwell made a face. "Keep it under five thousand if you can."

Kyle nodded. That wouldn't be hard. "Yes, sir."

"Oh, you know what?" Mrs. Gladwell said, a twinkle in her eye. "We can give Faith the credit card and she can go with him to buy everything. That way he won't have to wait for us to reimburse him."

Mr. Gladwell nodded. "Good idea."

They walked up to the house, and Kyle leaned against the truck door. Had they just offered to let their daughter go with him to shop for plants…like it was a date? Huh.

He grabbed a notebook and went to the backyard to sketch out some plans. Faith was waiting on the steps, having already changed into a pair of leggings and a T-shirt.

"Your parents just offered to send you plant shopping with me tomorrow."

She cocked her head. "You make it sound like they offered you a dowry and my hand in marriage."

A tiny thrill ran down his back. He walked over and stood a foot away from her. "What kind of dowry are we talking?"

She stood up slowly. "Two cows, a sheep, and four wheels of aged cheddar. Interested?"

He stroked his chin, considering. From her place on the first step, her eyes were even with his. They were deep brown, with flecks of gold around the pupils. Warm, kind eyes that swallowed you whole. "Four whole wheels of cheddar. That's a pretty good offer."

"I *am* the baby of the family. They won't marry me off to just anyone."

They stared at each other, smiling, and Kyle felt the flutter of nerves fire up in his stomach. Anyone else would call them butterflies, but he had too much experience blowing it at this point. He always did with girls. The nerves were a warning signal reminding him he needed to play it cool. That he was a fraud, and he shouldn't get in too deep. If he screwed this up, their little plan would crater before it got off the ground.

With effort, he took a step back. "Let's see how you are at selecting flowers, then I'll think about it."

She looked confused and a little hurt. Damn it, why couldn't he just *talk* to a girl without being a dumbass about it? He sighed. "Faith, are you absolutely sure about starting up this rumor?"

"Yes," she murmured.

This was going to end in pain, probably for both of them, but he couldn't say no…and he didn't want to. He hardly knew

Faith, but he knew Cameron, so if she was up for collateral damage, then so was he.

"I better get back to work," he said, avoiding her eyes.

"Hey! Where are you, gazelle?" a girl called from the side of the house. A moment later, a petite purple-haired hurricane in a white miniskirt and black tee blew into the backyard, then stopped short when she caught sight of Kyle. "Whoa. You're...*you*."

He choked back a laugh. "The last time I checked."

The girl was about as different from Faith as you could get—short, a force of nature, and as subtle as a sledgehammer. She looked him up and down like she was an agent auditioning male models. "Oh, it's definitely worth checking."

"Violet." Faith's voice held a hint of a chuckle—and a warning.

Violet rolled her blue eyes, striking in her pale face with the black and purple hair framing it. Like one of those miniature Goth dolls Cade's little sister had obsessed over when she was six. "Oh, come on. A guy does *not* work in your backyard all day half naked if he doesn't want you to do an inspection. But I seem to be making him blush."

She was, in fact. He fought it with all he had, but it was a losing battle. Violet's stare was like an X-ray. "Should I take off my shirt then?"

"Would you?" she asked cheerfully.

"Vi, stop." Faith sank down onto the porch steps, covering her face with her hands.

"I went too far again, huh?" Violet teetered over to the porch steps in platform sandals at a height between extreme and ridiculous. She plopped down next to Faith and rested her head on Faith's shoulder.

Faith shook her head, smiling ruefully, then shrugged. "Kyle, this is my best friend, Violet. She knows the plan."

Violet sat up straight, eyes gleaming. "And I

wholeheartedly approve. I will be your rumor mill, your publicist, your event planner. I'll need your number in case we need to plot or something. Seriously, though, name the task and I'm yours."

"Did I happen to mention that she's like a high-voltage battery?" Faith said, grinning at Kyle.

"Shocking and full of pent-up power?" he asked.

Faith looked pleased that he caught on so fast. "Exactly."

"Ooh, I like that." Violet laughed. "I'm stealing that one."

Looking at the two of them—one tall and warm with honey-colored skin and brown hair, the other tiny and all stark contrasts in black and white—they seemed like unlikely friends. Like he and Cade had been once.

"I like high-energy people," he said. "I've been accused of being too chill."

"Indeed. I couldn't tell," Violet said in a passable British accent. She turned to Faith and gripped her arm. "Girl, he's an amazing straight man. This is going to work."

"Yeah, it will," Faith said. She nodded at Kyle. "So let's start making plans."

Chapter Twelve

Kyle had a funny expression on his face. It was this cute, faint wrinkle to his forehead, and his eyes had widened, so the blue sparkled in the afternoon sun. Faith couldn't decide if he was confused, amused, or appalled. Then again, Violet tended to inspire all three in people, even guys who supposedly had seen it all.

Warmth filled her chest. How had she been so lucky to find a friend like her?

"So, I was thinking," Violet said. "And I told Faith about this, but you two need to make an appearance at Dolly's on Wednesday—a lot of people will be there then. I can find a way to make sure Cameron shows, too."

Faith hazarded a glance at Kyle, nervous. What if he decided the whole thing was stupid? From everything she'd heard, he didn't strike her as an "ice cream" kind of guy. Jack straight from the bottle maybe, not a chocolate chip cone with sprinkles. "If you don't want to…I mean, I know it's not your kind of place…"

"The drive-in?" He shrugged and picked up a rake. "I like a good shake now and then. That's fine with me. I have practice that afternoon, but I could do it in the evening."

What? He actually drank something other than malt liquor and Red Bull? "You've been there before?"

He turned to smile at her, and her neck grew warm. God, he had a nice smile, one that came out of nowhere and socked you between the eyes. He'd mastered the effect, for sure. This might be harder than she thought. What if she accidently developed more than a crush on him? She couldn't stand to be tossed aside twice.

And yet she was still blushing.

"*Everyone's* been there before," he was saying. "Why wouldn't it be my kind of place?"

"Because she thinks you hang out on dark street corners, smoking and playing with your switchblade," Violet pronounced.

Faith groaned. *And now I'm going to die of embarrassment. I won't even see the new backyard.*

Kyle leaned on the rake, studying her best friend. "You have a mouth on you."

"I've heard you do, too. *And* that you know how to use it," Violet said, standing up. "Fess up, hot boy. Tell me your secrets and I'll tell you mine."

His face turned bright pink, and he busied himself with raking up leaves, almost like Violet had frightened him. "I don't have any secrets."

"Which guarantees that you do." Violet hopped off the steps. "Girl, I like this one. He's multifunctional. There's depth there." She planted a kiss on top of Faith's head. "Just don't drown."

"Wait," Faith said, as Violet sauntered over to the gate. "You're *leaving*?"

"My work is done here." She glanced at Kyle, who stared uneasily back. "Dolly's, Wednesday. And Kyle? Start talking big to your friends about her. Make it good. But not too good. Save the big story for Thursday after everyone sees you. It'll require some acting, so maybe you two ought to practice actually looking like a couple. You know, try holding hands, kissing."

With a devilish smile and a wave, Violet disappeared around the corner of the house, but Faith could hear her cackling madly. Her cheeks flamed, probably turning the same color Kyle's had just been. Oh God, what had she done?

Swallowing down her embarrassment, Faith said, "Sorry. What can I say? She has no filters."

Kyle started raking up twigs and leaves left over from his attack on her shrubbery. "I kind of like that, actually. You know exactly where you stand with her."

Faith's embarrassment melted a little. "That's a nice thing to say. Most people don't get her right off."

He shot her that sweet smile again and she felt it in her knees. "My grandpa's a lot like that. You should hear the things that come out of his mouth." He chuckled. "He's crazy."

"And you love him," she blurted out. But it was the truth—she heard it in his voice, loud and clear and unembarrassed. Who exactly *was* Kyle Sawyer? The stories she knew didn't match the guy who tolerated Violet's smack talk and spoke kindly about his grandfather. Hell, half the people she knew figured he was an alien, dropped here to weigh and measure the population. The other half, mostly female, worshiped his biceps in secret, praying he might spare each of them an hour of his time.

And I'm slowly starting to fall in the second category. She picked at her fingernails, a little afraid of what he might really think of her, the good girl who went to church and doted on her cat. "Sorry. It just sounded…um…"

He turned away. "I do, actually. He and my dad are all I have. My mom died when I was young. It's just the three of us, and Grandpa raised me, pretty much."

"I'm sorry," she said softly.

Kyle attacked the yard with the rake, pulling up grass as he worked. "Don't be. It was a long time ago."

An awkward silence followed, begging to be filled. Faith rose from the step. "So, um, what Violet said. Uh, about the kissing thing. Don't feel like you have to…"

She trailed off and his shoulders bowed. "I wasn't. Not unless you ask."

A tiny breath escaped her mouth. Was he saying he would kiss her if she wanted him to? Not surprising—his kisses were cheap, apparently—but he sounded reluctant. Like he, for once, didn't want to kiss the girl right in front of him. Like she might not be worth the extra effort…and that stung.

She squashed her doubts down deep. This was business. He'd made his motivation for agreeing clear: to get back at Cameron for some past sin. "Are you going to tell me why you're willing to do this?"

The raking became even more violent. "I thought I did."

"You have a score to settle. From middle school."

"That's right." He paused to look at her, and his closed-off expression told her not to press.

"Okay. I'll quit bugging you while you work." She went to the back door, an ache burning in her chest, although she didn't know why. Why should she care about his demons? "I'll be ready to go shopping in the morning."

He didn't answer, and she wandered into the house. She really wanted to dance, and the smooth wood floors beneath her feet begged her to stay, but she needed to get away from Kyle and his chameleon moods. First sweet, then guarded, then dark, and she'd had enough of trying to figure out the right things to say around him.

Without a backward glance, she shut the porch door behind her, leaving Kyle alone to wrestle with his rake and his moods.

Chapter Thirteen

KYLE

The sound of the door being pushed shut seemed to echo for an entire minute. He just couldn't stop saying the wrong thing, could he? Every single time.

Kyle growled in frustration, hacking at the stubborn clump of Bermuda grass growing at the base of the Gladwells' big oak. He wanted to avoid spraying the grass with chemicals to kill it off, but it wouldn't let go, and he didn't have the time or patience to pull it all up.

Then again, now that Faith was in the house, he had nothing *but* time. He'd scared her away, and why? Because some hurts went too deep. He didn't want to open up about the time some kid had scrawled *fag* onto his locker door, or how Cameron's best friend had tripped him in the cafeteria, sending him—and his tray—reeling. Right into Rebecca Jamison, the girl he'd secretly liked for months, who'd ended up plastered with butterscotch pudding. She'd screamed at him in front of everyone, reducing him to a speck of nothing at her feet.

But it was talking about Grandpa that made too much feeling well up the back of his throat. After spending too many years avoiding it, vulnerability wasn't something he liked to show off in public. Especially in front of a cute girl with a rabid friend who'd been nothing but kind to him.

Unfortunately, now Faith thought he was mad at *her,* and he had no idea how to undo the damage. Was he always going to be that scared, scarred seventh grader inside? Would he figure out how to talk to a perfectly nice girl? She was exactly the kind of girl he daydreamed of meeting, but nothing he said worked out right.

Maybe he should stick to gardening and baseball. Those two things, he understood.

He put his earbuds in and went to work clearing out the last of the ornamentals that would have to go. By the time he finished, it was late afternoon and his back ached. Once again, hours had passed and he'd missed them all.

Neither Faith nor Mrs. Gladwell came out to tell him good-bye. It was just as well. He had one last chore to complete. He drove home and parked in the garage, but didn't get out. Time to start a wildfire—and he knew exactly who he'd hand the match to.

He pulled out his phone and texted Tristan. *Man, what's up?*

T: *Nothing much. You?*

Kyle sighed. This was it—the line was about to be crossed. No turning back now. *I met someone from Suttonville this weekend. She's hot. You know that Faith Gladwell girl? Dancer?*

T: *Yeah. 'Course I know her. She was Cameron's girlfriend. Heard she wouldn't put out. Not your type.*

K: *Really? She seemed pretty into me yesterday. You know me—I'll take a rebound. Lots of fun and they don't stay long.*

T: *You're gonna hit that? Bullshit.*

K: *Twenty bucks says I am. By the time we go back to school.*

T: *Dude, you're on. Easiest twenty bucks ever.*

Kyle winced. Tristan didn't need the cash, but he'd lose this bet based on Kyle's lie. But that's what he did—lied. Unfortunately, he'd become very good at it.

He went inside. Dad and Grandpa were laughing about something in the living room. The sounds of a hockey game played in the background, and the scent of pizza lured him forward.

"Look who's home!" Dad crowed, toasting his arrival with a beer.

Dorky as it might be, a rush of affection overtook him. At home, people were glad to see him, which helped when the welcome wasn't as kind at school. "Any pizza left for me?"

"Bought you a medium supreme so you wouldn't have to share," Grandpa said. "Figured you'd be as starved as a wolf pup after working all day."

"You're my favorite grandpa," Kyle said. "I'm going to shower. Down in five."

"He's your only grandpa," Dad called after him.

Maybe, but it didn't make it any less true.

The next morning, Kyle showed up at the Gladwells' house

promptly at nine, wearing clothes a little too nice for gardening. It wasn't like taking Faith flower shopping was a date, but he'd had a sudden urge to look decent when considering a pair of ratty cargo shorts and a T-shirt with a hole in the underarm. He'd gone to his closet, realizing he had *way* too much black in his wardrobe. For some reason, that hadn't cut it, either.

So here he was, in a pair of khaki shorts, a dark blue Polo and a pair of Sperrys without socks, feeling more and more self-conscious as he waited for the door to open. He hadn't dressed this preppy in town in years. The outfit was from vacation last summer, when Dad insisted that he have "nice restaurant on the beach" attire for their trip to the Florida Keys. Grandpa had choked on his Mountain Dew when Kyle wore the outfit the first time.

And now he was wearing it again. He'd thrown the ratty shorts and T-shirt into a drawstring backpack to change into later, but what would Faith think about his clothes?

He paused. When had he started worrying about how he looked around her? It wasn't like they were dating. Not really. Right? He stared at her front door, hoping he wasn't making a giant mistake. Shaking his head, he pushed the doorbell.

No one answered. He rang again. Nothing.

He checked the time on his phone: 9:02. Okay, what was taking her so long? She had to be here—the only car in their driveway was a yellow Volkswagen Bug with those silly accessory eyelashes on the headlights. If that wasn't Faith's car, he'd eat his shoe.

He raised his hand to knock, in case the bell was broken, just as Faith flung it open. Now he could see why it had taken her a minute. Her hair was damp, and she had on wrinkled PJ shorts and a tank top.

Her cheeks turned pink after she took a look at him. "Sorry—I overslept."

"It happens," he said, distracted by the miles of bare leg

those shorts left uncovered. "Um, I can wait out here if you want."

"No, no, come in," she said, waving him inside. "You look…nice."

She said it like a question and he bit back a smile. "You say that like you're surprised."

"It's just…" She frowned, peering at him. "You usually wear a lot of black. And a hoodie."

Now it was his turn to flush. Maybe he shouldn't have made such an effort. "Only to school."

She led him through an entry with a staircase into a living room made homey with soft leather furniture, hand-scraped wood floors, and a piano in the corner. "You play?" he asked.

"No, I sing, mostly. Joy—my older sister—plays."

The smile he'd been trying to swallow came back full force. "Joy. Faith and *Joy*?"

She rolled her eyes. "And Hope. Hope, Joy, and Faith Gladwell. Our parents hate us."

That eye roll—a good-natured weariness over the joke of her name—broke something inside him. What was it with this girl? So much humor and sweetness and talent in one person wasn't something you found every day. Maybe there was some magic in the name her parents had chosen. "I'd say the opposite. Naming their kids Hope, Joy, and Faith? They love you, I think." He snorted. "They always could've named you Grace, Patience, and Chastity."

"I think those are implied," she said, smiling a little herself.

"Which one of those three are you?" he said, his voice going deeper, husky, of its own accord.

Her shoulders slumped. "You know what Cameron would say."

"Unfortunately, everyone knows what Cameron would say." He took a step toward her, keeping his eyes fixed on her face. "But what about you?"

"I'd love to say Grace, but maybe once you get to know me, you can decide for yourself," she murmured. "I'm going to run upstairs and change. Make yourself at home."

She dashed toward the entry, and a moment later, he heard her pounding up the stairs. "You don't have to rush on my account," he called. "We have time."

"Yes, but I hate being late!" she called back.

That didn't surprise him. He wandered through the living room. Every surface was covered with family photos, and dozens of tiny Faiths smiled at him from every direction. Dance photos from recitals. Christmas mornings. School pictures. And, on the back wall, three senior photos, one of each sister. All of them were pretty, but Faith had a shine to her the other two lacked, something that said, "I'm special. You'll like me." More proof Cameron was a raging ass. This girl wasn't someone you walked away from. She was fast becoming the kind of girl *he'd* have trouble walking away from.

Shaking his head, Kyle went through the kitchen and let himself out on the back porch. A cool breeze blew through the screen windows and the wood floor creaked under his feet. It was worn and painted smooth. The rail he'd seen Faith stretching on yesterday turned out to be a real ballet barre. It was only five feet long, but definitely the real deal. He ran his hand along it—the wood was worn smooth here, too. This was a place she spent a lot of time.

"Kyle?"

He jumped and hurried back inside. "Sorry—I was just, uh, checking on my mess in the backyard."

Faith had changed into leggings, a pair of ripped jean shorts, and a pink T-shirt that said, "Ballet dancers do it on their toes," in white script letters.

"What is that shirt?" he asked, unable to keep from chuckling.

She smoothed it out, her shoulders bunching around her ears. "Something stupid Violet bought me as a gag gift for my birthday. I've always been too embarrassed to wear it, but I thought today… I'll just go change."

She turned to go, but he held out a hand. "No, wait. You should wear it. It's pretty funny given what we're trying to do. New rule: I promise not to laugh at any of your outfits, as long as you stop giving a shit what people think. Deal?"

She stood, back straight, shoulders thrown out. *Owning* that shirt. "Deal."

"Then let's go." He pulled his keys out of his pocket. "Time to show ourselves around town."

Chapter Fourteen

Faith's cheeks still burned after Kyle's initial reaction to the T-shirt. It really was kind of stupid, but, as he put it, it made sense. She was proving a point, and the T-shirt helped with that. The reason the blowup with Cameron hurt so much wasn't that he'd cheated on her, but he'd let the whole school in on it, knowing how much it would get to her. Funny how Kyle could remind her it didn't matter. That she needed to be her own person. It was hard, though.

She followed him out of the house and turned to lock the front door, giving herself time to take a few breaths. It was so strange having him over, actually inside. And that outfit—he looked like a completely different person. Nicer.

Boyfriend material.

She shook that thought off. He might be the cutest guy she'd been around—maybe ever—but they were in this situation to get a reaction, not become a couple. So what if she'd caught him running his hand over her ballet barre on the porch, like it amazed him. Or the way he stared at her—all honesty, no bullshit. If this is who he really was, she had no idea why so many people at school, especially guys, gave him so much space.

"You coming?" he called.

She jumped, realizing she'd taken way too long to put her key in the lock. "Um, yeah."

The little Toyota pickup at the curb was nothing like the Charger she normally saw him drive. It was a faded red, dented, and had a hubcap missing on the back tire. It was the kind of truck landscapers drove, sure, but would it make it around the block?

He held the door open for her, eyebrow raised. What, did he think she was too good to ride around with him? Head held high, she marched down the flagstone sidewalk and climbed into the truck without a word.

He snorted when he closed the door, and only then did it dawn on her—he'd held it open for her. Heat flooded her face, all the way to the roots of her hair. "Thanks for opening my door."

The grin he gave her sent goose bumps racing up her arms. "I pull out all the stops when I'm aiding and abetting a revenge-seeking ex-girlfriend."

That wasn't exactly the vibe *she* was getting, and she couldn't decide whether to be concerned or intrigued. Was he trying to seduce her for real? Or was he simply a great actor?

Not knowing was part of the fun.

"So, Little Red here." She patted the dashboard as the engine sputtered to life. "Does the Charger get jealous when you drive another car?"

"What, you don't like her?" Kyle tsked and shook his head. "We can't be friends, then."

"Are we?" Faith blurted out. "Friends?"

She wanted to eat the words as soon as they came out of

her mouth, but the look Kyle leveled at her was thoughtful, and way too serious. "That's up to you."

She nodded slowly. "Okay, friends, then. But that means you have to tell me a secret."

"Will you tell me one?" he asked, glancing at her as they drove out of the neighborhood and onto the main street into town.

"You already know one," she said. "Our deal is my secret."

"It's mine, too, then." The corner of his mouth twitched. "Unless you're willing to give me something new."

She slumped in her seat, marveling at how quickly Kyle outmaneuvered her. "Fine. What do you want to know?"

"Something really weird," he said, that stupid half smirk still on his face.

"Do you really want to know, or are you pushing my buttons?"

"Both."

"I believe it." Faith racked her brain for something weird, but not *weird*. Nothing came to mind, except that she ate peanut butter on her pancakes instead of syrup. God, she was so boring.

"Nothing?" He shot her this incredulous look. "Seriously, *nobody* is that normal."

His teasing expression caught her off guard. He had such a *nice* smile for a delinquent. Her brain took over, and next thing she knew, "I can eat with my feet…using a fork," came flying out of her mouth.

Oh, for the love of Bob Fosse, she did *not* just admit that.

"That sounds….uncomfortable." Amusement colored his tone. "What would make you want to try that?"

Her shoulders rounded and she wrapped her arms around her middle. Stupid, stupid, stupid. "I was testing to see how flexible I was."

His mouth dropped open slightly. He snapped it closed.

"I know it's weird, but I didn't expect you to laugh at me." She turned to stare out the window. "I'm not sure I like this game."

He sighed. "I wasn't laughing."

"Forget I said it, okay? It's my stupid human trick, nothing else."

"I wasn't laughing," he said again, his voice soft. "I wouldn't do that to you." They turned into the parking lot at the nursery, and gravel crunched under the Toyota's tires, kicking up rocks and making enough noise that she didn't have to say anything else right away. When they parked, Kyle turned off the ignition and sat with one hand on the steering wheel. A muscle ticked in his jaw.

"I'm not very good at this," he said.

"At what?"

He stared straight ahead. "Being friends. With girls."

"Yeah, right." Faith reached for the door handle, but he put a hand on her arm.

"That's my secret. You told me one, so I told you one." His smile was tight, and fainter than the ones before. "I'm not what you'd consider a conversationalist."

Was he kidding?

She met his gaze, eyes narrowed. "So, what, you're just good at picking the right girl to hook up with and she runs off with you as soon as you jerk your chin at her?"

He shook his head, eyes rolled toward the sky. "Not exactly. And just so you know, you might have to help me decipher some signs inside. I'm dyslexic." He flung his door open and climbed out. Faith scurried after him. "That's not a secret, but it's not something I talk about, either. Good enough?"

A pit of embarrassment opened up in her stomach. She hadn't meant to force him to tell her that. "Sure."

The nursery was a large greenhouse set on an acreage

that offered baby trees and paving stones. It smelled delicious. Like spring had exploded into bloom all around her. Her eyes stung for a moment, remembering the ride to Violet's a few days ago. Cameron always thought she was being "a girl" and sentimental about this stuff, but she'd been thinking about rebirth then, and it had happened. Now she could move forward and think about growth. Change.

Moving forward.

"You okay?"

Faith jumped. She'd really lost the thread there, hadn't she? "What? Sorry."

Kyle had stopped his march to the greenhouse door, and he watched her with his eyebrows drawn together. "You seemed sad just now. I'm really not laughing about the fork thing, if you're thinking that. I hate it when people laugh at other people's expense."

The worry in his voice was another thing that reminded her of Cameron—because Cameron had never worried about pissing her off. Kyle obviously did. "It wasn't that at all. I was just thinking…I really love spring. I know that's stupid."

"It's not stupid. If you love watching things grow, it's the best time of year." He held the door open for her. "You coming?"

Warmth rushed through her. "Yeah. Definitely."

Chapter Fifteen

KYLE

Kyle took a deep breath as soon as they entered the nursery, hoping the smell of green things growing would relax the knot in his shoulders. Why had he told Faith the truth about talking to girls? What was she thinking out there, staring out at the trees? She'd looked so torn, but hopeful, and sad, too. What did he *say*?

Admitting the dyslexia was the only thing he could think of to change the subject. *Way to go, jerk—making her feel guilty for your mistake.*

"This place is awesome!" Faith breezed past him, heading straight for the flowers. She didn't look upset anymore, wearing a bright smile. She glided toward the rows of annuals. "These pink ones are so pretty!"

He came alongside her, relieved he hadn't done any lasting damage. "Those are vinca. I'm planning to get some— they bloom early and keep going until late fall. Something an ex-governor's wife might like, right?"

"Definitely." She bounced over to the next table, running her fingers along a gray-green leaf. The little plant swayed at her touch. "What's this?"

"Dusty miller. Good ground cover. It can get out of control, but you have a good lawn guy. He'll make sure it behaves."

She laughed behind her hand. She always did that, like his jokes were a surprise, and it put a smile back on his face. Faith found joy in the simplest things. She seemed a little fragile to him, but that could be the hurt from the last few days. Maybe if he could make her laugh enough she'd forget about Cameron all together.

He followed her up the aisle, pointing out plants that would go well in their backyard, taking care to listen when she had a doubt. If she didn't approve of it, her mom probably wouldn't, either.

"I like this one," Faith murmured. Her fingers skimmed the tiny pink flowers dotting the plant's thin branches.

Kyle reached out and brushed his hand along hers as he grasped a section of leaves. Faith stiffened for a second, but didn't move her hand. He was standing behind her, and something made him take a step forward so that his chest was almost touching her back. His knees trembled a little, but his voice was level when he said, "Azalea. They're beautiful, and while they look delicate, they're strong if they're taken care of the right way. They're perfect for you."

She held very still. "You think?"

He swallowed hard. Praying she didn't notice that his hand was shaking now, too, he brushed his lips against her ear, saying. "Absolutely."

"Are we still talking about plants?"

There was something coy to her tone, and it unnerved him, which was stupid, since he knew she could flirt. "I'm not sure."

She ducked out from under his arm, smiling. "Trouble talking to girls, he says. Uh-huh. Sure."

Kyle flushed and took a step back. "We're still, uh, buying the azaleas, right?"

"Yep."

She wandered up another aisle, and he let out a slow breath. She'd never believe him if he told her the truth, would she? He'd told her he wasn't good at talking to girls and she didn't believe it. How would she react if she knew the truth about the "real" Kyle Sawyer?

Probably twirl over and kick him in the nuts.

Besides, if the plan with Cameron was going to work, she didn't need to know any more than she already did. It was enough that he had to act a part. He couldn't be sure she'd be able to keep it up if she knew.

"I found a couple more!" Faith called. "Will you come see if they'll work?"

He forced himself to loosen up and let the swagger creep back in. "On my way."

"That's a lot of plants," Faith said, staring at the pots and buckets littering the backyard.

"It's less than you think." Kyle dragged the six azaleas over to the shady part of the yard. He'd see to it these lived, if nothing else did. There wasn't much he could do to impress Faith, but if this did, he'd work for it.

"Oh, I'm sure. You made a pretty big pile of ripped out bushes earlier." She twirled a strand of hair around her finger.

What would her hair feel like against his fingers? He knew her hair smelled like citrus, but he wouldn't mind running his fingers through it to see if it was as silky as it looked. And she was warm, too. When he stood behind her at the store, he could feel her body heat. And those legs…

Oh, shit.

No, no, no—this could not happen. She was a pretty girl, that's all. Faith had too many good things ahead of her without him in the picture. And wasn't that getting ahead of himself? She'd never want someone like him. She deserved better than a liar who was too scared to admit what scared him.

"You in there?" she asked, startling him. He had the feeling she'd kept talking, and he hadn't heard a word.

"Um, yeah. Sorry, I was planning out where to put everything."

She raised an eyebrow. "Yeah—and that's what I was asking. You okay?"

"Fine." The word came out a lot rougher than he intended, and Faith stepped back like he'd taken a swing at her.

"Okay," she said slowly. "Guess I'll leave you to it."

She turned and went inside, casting a quizzical look over her shoulder. Kyle leaned against the big tree and banged the back of his head against the bark He was messing this up, and it wasn't even a real thing. Why did she wind him up so much? He'd been paid to do a job, not get involved with the girl who lived here.

Cursing under his breath, he starting laying out the rest of the garden.

Chapter Sixteen

Of all the infuriating… Faith climbed upstairs to her room, hardly noticing how she got there. What was going on with her and Kyle? Every so often, she thought he might actually be warming up to her, then he closed down. She'd thought he'd be the exact opposite—trying to charm his way into her tights with everything he had—but he kept going cold on her. Was she really that boring, not worth his time? God, how could she live knowing she wasn't good enough for Kyle Sawyer? *Everyone* was supposedly good enough for him.

Sure he was cute, but was it worth being toyed with? Or constantly wondering what would make him close off?

Not even. Maybe she should call off the whole plan.

But that moment at the nursery…when he'd stood right behind her. She'd made a joke about it, thinking then he was just playing her. After she had time to think about it, and how quiet he'd been on the way home, she had to wonder. The plan aside, what did she *really* know about Kyle? Were his shifting moods about something else?

She paced around the room, staying away from the window so she wouldn't be tempted to check on him, thinking about all the things that didn't add up. First, there was the way he treated his pickup. That truck was close to a calamity, but he coaxed it into running like a patient dad with a temperamental toddler. Granted, he needed it for work, but he didn't have the reputation of being gentle with vehicles. The word at school was he tortured his Charger, drag racing down Mill Road on the weekends.

Was that even true?

And what about the rumor he had a pack-a-day habit? She'd seen zero evidence of cigarettes anywhere, not even a whiff on his clothes. He played baseball, and was supposedly really good. Why would an athlete risk his body like that? Oh, sure, she knew tons of dancers who smoked, but that was because they were starving themselves for a part. She didn't know any athletes who did—and she knew most of the football and track teams, thanks to Cameron.

There were also rumors about shoplifting, graffiti, and general hooliganism, but where was the evidence?

Who was Kyle Sawyer?

She tapped a finger against her lips. Violet worked in the school office during third period. Could she look up his record, see if he'd ever been suspended? Because he disappeared once or twice a year, and everyone suspected he was doing in-school suspension. What if it that wasn't true? What if he'd been sick or gone on a vacation? None of this was making sense.

Flopping down on her bed, she fished her phone from her pocket to text Vi and ask, then sat up again fast. Sweet Mother of Unicorns, there were eighteen—*eighteen*—texts on her phone.

Fifteen of them were from girls at school, all along the

lines of, "You'll never guess what I heard!" and "Is it true? Seriously?"

There were two messages from Violet: *Girl! It's out—I don't know how he did it, but I'm hearing from everyone.*

V: *You're officially Kyle's new girl-of-the-week! It's all over the senior class.*

The last text was from Cameron: *You hold me off for months, now you're hooking up with that asshole? I was only with Holly because you hurt me. You don't have to throw it in my face like this.*

A grim smile spread across her face. Maybe being toyed with was worth it after all.

Chapter Seventeen

KYLE

Kyle went after the flower bed like he had a personal vendetta against it. The Texas clay was hard after being half frozen all winter, and it really didn't want to break up. Good thing, because he needed an outlet, and this saved his knuckles from punching the wall. Coach would have a fit if he broke his fingers two weeks before their next game.

Idiot. Dumbass. Coward. Those three words pounded his brain in a relentless circle. *Idiot. Dumbass. Coward.* He never should've agreed to this plan with Faith. He had too much to lose. And now? Now he was in danger of letting her in. He *couldn't* do that.

He wanted to.

Idiot.

God, how he wanted to.

Dumbass.

But he was too scared.

Coward.

Kyle slammed his spade into the flower bed and rubbed a grubby hand over his face. What was he going to do? His lies were piled so high, they were going to topple over any minute, and he wasn't sure he could stop them. After carefully creating his persona, he was in danger of destroying it. Worse, this plan called for something he wasn't. Faith wanted a guy with experience.

What if she found out he had exactly zero?

"Kyle!" The screen door banged open and Faith flew down the steps. She skidded to a halt five feet away and started laughing. "Um, if I weren't such a nice person, I'd snap a picture of you right now."

"Why?" he asked, tired. Even if his lies made his bones ache, her smile sparked all kinds of impossible dreams. Maybe…

"Because your face is covered in dirt. It's…" She reached out a hand like she was going to wipe it away, then drew it back, blushing. "It's adorable, actually."

A grin slowly tugged its way across his face, despite his best efforts to stop it. "I must look like a mess."

"Yes, but according to the eighteen texts I just read, you're *my* mess," she said triumphantly. "How did you do it? How did you make them believe we're…uh…we're…"

Her face turned bright pink, and his confidence returned. "Having crazy sex?"

"Yeah, that." She stared at the azaleas planted in a neat line near the fence. "Those are beautiful."

"They'll look better once they root. So you're okay? Now that it's out?"

"I am. Cameron is pissed." They shared matching, hard smiles. "Thank you."

"Don't mention it." *Say something, moron! Ask her out. Don't let this go to waste.*

Weird how his thoughts were rooting him on in Grandpa's

voice. But he was right—for once he needed to get over his fear of letting someone in and make a move.

He swallowed against the tide of nerves boiling in his stomach. "I think that calls for a celebration, though, don't you?"

She cocked her head, and he couldn't keep from staring at her long, smooth neck. "What do you have in mind?"

This was it. *Don't screw this up.* "It's a surprise. Tomorrow night? Eight o'clock? I promise you'll be back by ten, in case you have a curfew."

"My curfew's midnight." She was blushing again. "So if we decide to stay out later, that won't be a problem."

"Yeah, but your parents are my clients, so I don't want to piss them off before the job's done."

She laughed. "Good plan. My dad was an Olympic archer way back in the day. Probably best not to piss him off…like, ever."

"Good to know." He picked up his spade. "Tomorrow then."

"Tomorrow."

Once she skipped back into the house—*really* skipped— he leaned against the spade's handle. Could this be it? Could she be the one?

He hoped so.

That night, after a shower and a lot of Neosporin for the cuts on his hands—azaleas bite, apparently—he went down for dinner. Grandpa was already at the table, dressed in a bright orange golf shirt and matching pants.

"Ouch, are you trying to blind me?" Kyle asked, taking his seat. "What's with the neon?"

"I like to be visible on the golf course, in case some idiot forgets it's not hunting season." Grandpa pushed a paper bag his way. "Burgers from McCallen's. Rosanna has bingo tonight, and your dad's working late."

"Fine by me." Kyle dived into his cheeseburger and fries. The date had him nervous—what would they talk about for two whole hours? He had a plan for where to take her, but beyond that, he was totally stuck. "Grandpa?"

"Yup?" He barely looked up from his onion rings, but Kyle didn't care. McCallen rings were a religious experience.

"Um, I'm taking this girl out tomorrow."

Grandpa's head whipped up, half a ring dangling from his hand. "Say what?"

Oh, for the love of… "You heard me, old man."

He chuckled. "I was just wondering if maybe I needed a hearing aid after all. So, you're actually taking a girl out—and telling me about it?" He set his onion ring down. "You have my full attention."

"I'll talk fast, because I don't want the blame if your rings are too cold to eat. Anyway, it's this girl from school I was telling you about yesterday."

"Is she pretty? Is she nice? Does she have nice parents? Does she get good grades?"

Kyle laughed. "I *knew* I shouldn't have said anything. I knew you'd freak out."

Grandpa held up a hand. "I promise to stop. I'm really proud of you, kid."

"Yeah. About that…I have no idea what to talk to her about for two whole hours."

"Aw, that's easy." Grandpa went back to his onion rings. "What does she like to do for fun?"

Date stupid football players? Run around with a purple-haired sprite? "She likes to dance. I heard her say something about the school musical."

That perked him up. "Which one?"

Kyle shrugged. "How should I know?"

Grandpa rolled his eyes and pointed his onion ring at him. "Maybe ask? Or better yet—ask someone she knows. That way you can surprise her with small talk."

Okay, some of that made a little sense. "I can do that."

"Good. Text the friend, then finish your dinner. We have plans."

Uh-oh. When Grandpa said they had plans, it was definitely smart to worry. Still, Kyle texted Violet, wondering what the old man was up to.

Two minutes later: *Oklahoma! Duh—there are posters all over school. Why do you want to know?*

He frowned at his phone. What would she believe? *Because I need to know some things about Faith if anybody on the team asks me about her. Duh.*

She sent an emoji with its tongue wagging out, and that was the last he heard. "She's in *Oklahoma!* If I had to guess, she'll be the lead."

"Perfect!" Grandpa crumbled his sandwich wrapper and tossed into the paper sack. "Finish your dinner, then come to my den."

Kyle did as he asked, grumbling the whole time, then went to Grandpa's den—a wood-paneled man cave with well-worn leather furniture, a two-month-old flat-screen TV, and a sixty-year-old vinyl collection. Kyle had always loved this room. Leather couches so old and soft they were nearly falling apart. A dartboard, complete with holes in the wall from when he was little and couldn't hit the target. Tin signs, collected from flea markets and yard sales, going back to the 1920s. This part of the house didn't feel like the rest, which meant it didn't look like it belonged in a ten-thousand-square-foot home in The Hills subdivision. Maybe that's why Kyle loved it—the room was real. Lived-in.

Honest.

A guy started singing, startling him out of his thoughts. A cowboy in a shirt too clean to make him legit was singing something about corn and elephant's eyes. "Oh, don't tell me…"

"Yep, this one's a doozy. *Oklahoma!* looks innocent, but there's a lot of innuendo. We're going to watch the *whole* thing." Grandpa had a twinkle in his eyes. "That way, you can speak intelligently about the most important thing on this young lady's mind. She'll love it. I promise."

Kyle settled onto the couch. "Part of me wonders if we're doing this so you can torture me."

"And you'd be right." Grandpa grinned at him. "But I'm right about the other thing, too."

"Okay." As he watched, a grandma traded barbs with the cowboy, then a pretty blond girl came out of the farmhouse and started singing with them. "Is that the lead?"

"Yeah, that's Laurey. That'll be your girl's part." Grandpa squeezed his shoulder. "I thought you might run out on me as soon it started. You must like this girl a lot to endure watching a whole musical with me."

Kyle stared at his hands, remembering the way he felt standing close to Faith at the nursery. Like he'd been electrified. Like the only thing that mattered was making her happy. "You know what? I think I might."

Chapter Eighteen

He asked me out. He asked me out? Faith couldn't decide if it was a statement or a question. It sure seemed like he asked her out, discussing curfew and a surprise, but should she assume that?

Because she sure wanted to.

Kyle, who had a habit of being frustrating as hell, seemed genuinely interested in her, not just as a girl or an assignment, but as a person. A few hours ago she wouldn't have thought that, but things had become a lot clearer after he asked her out (did he?). She didn't know how she knew, but the way he looked at her mattered. Cameron's gaze had always been predatory, possessive. Kyle's was surprisingly shy, but also like he wanted to understand what made her tick. It made her feel…things she probably shouldn't be feeling if she wasn't sure if his surprise was a date or not.

God, why did this guy have her so confused? She barely knew him.

In fact, she wasn't sure she knew him at all. This whole day did nothing but contradict everything she'd ever heard about him. She knew he wore black T-shirts and hoodies with the hood up and earbuds in to school, but what about the rest of it? The smoking? She was sure that was a rumor someone made up for no reason, but why would he let that rumor linger? She'd quash it in a second if someone said that about her.

Except…wasn't she was doing the same thing to get back at Cameron? Yeah, maybe she didn't have the right to question anything.

Her stomach had been in knots since Kyle left, and she couldn't stand the tug anymore. She picked up her phone and dialed Vi, blurting out, "I think Kyle asked me out," before Vi could say anything.

There was a long pause. "Hmm. Interesting. Did you say yes?"

"Well, yeah. I was so shocked by the whole thing, I just kind of nodded like a doofus before I could really think it over."

"I'm proud of you. Getting back on the horse so soon." Vi's laugh was wicked. "Or on something else. Kyle looks like he'd be nice to straddle."

Faith flushed all over, trying to block the image from stamping itself across her brain. Losing battle, that. "Vi!"

"Oh, come on. What if the best revenge isn't just a rumor? I like Kyle for you. Every girl should have one bad boy in her life."

"That's just it. I'm not sure he really *is* bad. I mean, the whole smoking rumor? I haven't seen him smoke once while he's been working over here. And I don't smell cigarettes on his clothes or in his car."

"Maybe he quit?"

"Or maybe he never started." Faith sighed. "He's a puzzle."

"That makes it even better. Hot body, sexy car, mysterious past—what more could you want in a guy?"

Answers. "Guess I'll find out."

Once Vi told her exactly what to wear, she ended the call and went downstairs. A pot of chicken chili bubbled on the stove, filling the kitchen with the scent of chipotle. Her knotted stomach relaxed, letting out a small growl. Her mom's cooking had that effect on even the most stubborn butterflies.

She gave the chili a stir. Where was everyone? "Mom?"

"Out here!"

She rounded the corner to the screened-in porch. Mom was sitting in her favorite chair, a mug of coffee in hand, staring out at the backyard. "He really does beautiful work, doesn't he?"

Faith turned and drew in a sharp breath. Working with Kyle, she'd only really looked at the details—plant this flat of flowers here, arrange this ground cover there. But now she saw the whole backyard. Sure, it wasn't done: dirt mounds lined the back of the fence and the grass was still patchy, turning brown where he'd sprayed it with something to make it easier to pull up. The parts he'd finished, though, were perfect. The little flower garden on the right side of the yard, setting off the new bushes, added color against the fence. And the little copse of azaleas was a riot of pinks, reds, and whites. There was even an antique metal garden table and chair she didn't recognize. She had no idea where they came from, but they added a little touch of old-style romance to the flower side of the fence.

She covered her mouth with her hand. It was gorgeous. "When we bought all those plants this morning, I had no idea it would look like this. He's really good."

Mom gave her a sly look. "Yes, he is. And we're robbing the kid blind. He's charging me half of what a landscaping company would." She chuckled. "I'll have to make sure to throw in a good bonus."

"I think he'd like that, but it's more that he enjoys the work." Faith settled on the old sofa next to Mom. It was almost unreal how good Kyle's eye was for color and design. "He really loves it."

Mom shot her a sidelong glance. "You sure seem to know him well for having just met him. Anything I need to know about?"

Faith dropped her gaze to her hands. A little dirt was still stuck under one of her nails. "He, uh, kind of asked me out today."

"Did he now?" Faith could hear the smile in Mom's tone. "Well, he seems like a good kid. If I can trust him with my backyard, I suppose I can trust him to take my daughter out." She paused. "Or did you say no?"

If Mom only knew what they said about him at school, she wouldn't be so okay with it. But Faith decided *she* was. "I said yes. We'll go out tomorrow after he's done for the day."

"Good."

She hoped. Maybe she'd get more out of this bargain with Kyle than she'd imagined.

The next morning, Faith went to the studio to practice for the big dance scenes in the musical. Full cast rehearsal started next week, and she wanted to be the most prepared member there. For all her confidence once she had an audience, it was hard to be "on" during rehearsals. She second-guessed every step, every note. The dream sequence would be the most difficult piece. She hoped Josh, the guy playing Jud, was practicing, too. He had to lift her three times, and they hadn't danced together yet.

And it was a good excuse to avoid Kyle. For some reason,

now that they were going on a date, being home while he was there made her feel self-conscious. Stupid—it was *her* house, after all—but the thought of watching him work sent a wave of nerves down her spine to prickle against the back of her knees. She worried about being attracted to him, not wanting to date another guy who saw her as disposable. Somehow, though, she was having a hard time believing that. Not with the way he looked at her. Either he was better at seducing girls than she thought, or she was special.

Wouldn't that be something…wonderful?

"I'm going out for lunch, dear," Madame called from the doorway to the small studio. Even at forty, she was still elegant and lean in the leotard she'd covered with a long flowing skirt and open button-down shirt. "You interested in picking up a preschool ballet lesson at two?"

"Sure." Faith whirled around, trying to ignore the ache in her toes from standing en pointe.

"Any word from NYU?"

She paused in her routine and shook her head. Her pulse tripped in her veins. "They said they'd send out final responses sometime next week. I'm a little scared."

Madame walked into the room and took her hands. "I watched you record that audition video. You're good enough, honey. And if they pass, their loss…but I doubt they'll pass."

Anxiety flared in Faith's stomach. She'd worked so hard for this chance. It was her dream, her future, on the line. "I hope not."

Madame released her hands. "Don't worry. Good things are coming for you. I have a feeling."

She left the studio, but Faith stood frozen for a minute. Good things. Last weekend had been horrible, but maybe the rest of the week would fix all that, and in the end, she'd have her acceptance letter, too. Squaring her shoulders, Faith went to the stereo and put on the track for the hoedown scene.

Chapter Nineteen

KYLE

The Toyota rattled its way home. Kyle's hands ached from hoeing and tearing at the grass in the Gladwells' yard, and he feared the dirt crusted under his nails was a permanent addition. Not exactly the impression he wanted to make with Faith tonight, especially since she hadn't been home to see what he was working on. She might assume he was lazy.

Or a slob.

The familiar tug of nerves tried to claw its way up his throat. Damn it, not this time. This time he'd have a date with a nice, pretty girl, and he wouldn't fuck it up. He wouldn't.

Feeling defiant, he turned into the driveway and parked in the standalone garage next to Grandpa's Benz. Dad's car was gone, but it was only five thirty, and it was tax season.

He unloaded the truck and carried everything to the workshop at the back of the garage Dad had set up for him as a reward for starting his business. They didn't need room for six cars, and Kyle enjoyed the quiet the workshop gave him.

Kyle took his time cleaning his tools, bending at the waist every so often to stretch the kinks from his back. Where had Faith been all day? Her car was there when he started work, but gone when he went to lunch, and still gone when he stopped for the day. Had she decided to back out of their date and hidden instead?

His stomach clenched again. Good-bye, defiance—now he was nervous.

He wiped his damp hands on his filthy jeans and loaded his tools back into the Toyota. The truck was sloppy with mud and dead plant matter. No way he could show up for a date in it, even if he wanted to, just to stop being a jackass poseur for a minute. However, on the other side of the garage, the Charger gleamed in the fluorescent light. A smile spread across his face. He didn't remember it being so clean this morning when he left for work. Kyle might be a poseur, but his grandpa knew what impressed the ladies.

"I'm home!" he hollered from the mudroom after kicking his mud-caked boots off by the door.

"In here!" Grandpa's voice came from the kitchen.

Kyle went to the fridge. Grandpa was sitting at the table, reading glasses perched at the end of his nose. He was reading one of those men's magazines—the article read "Get Shredded in Thirty Days."

Kyle swallowed a laugh. "Thinking about working out?"

Grandpa snorted. "I don't understand a word of this. In my day, you ran two miles, did forty sit-ups, forty push-ups, twenty pull-ups, and called it good. This here says I'm supposed to have a chest day, a leg day, an arm and shoulders day. Who has the time?"

"Uh, you? You are retired, you know."

"Poppycock. You take a look at the Charger?"

He smiled. "Yeah. Thanks for having her washed."

"Hey, can't take a lady for a ride around town in a dirty

car, son. This tells her she's special." The corner of Grandpa's mouth twitched. "And I'm assuming that's true since you sat through the whole musical last night."

"And I've had that Kansas City song stuck in my head since." He took a swig from his water bottle. "Drove me nuts."

"Those men could dance back then." Grandpa's tone was approving. "Hmm, wonder if your date is a girl who just cain't say no?"

Kyle's ears flamed up. "Jesus, Grandpa. I'm not dating Ado Annie."

"Well, I can hope, right?" His grin softened. "You're a good kid. You got more of me than your Daddy in you, so naturally I believe that. Don't let yourself get in the way tonight, and this Faith girl will see it, too."

"I know." He toyed with his bottle cap. "It's just been a while since I tried this hard."

"And you've been lonely." Grandpa's sigh was heavy. "I know I'm partly at fault for that, but maybe it's time to let your guard down a little."

Kyle's palms grew slick with sweat. "Maybe."

"It'll be fine. Hear me? You're okay, kid. You are. That incident before ninth grade with what's her name from camp? That's history."

"You call it an incident, I call it a crash and burn." Kyle could still remember Cara's face when he took her for a moonlit stroll down to the canoe dock and made his move so badly she wouldn't speak to him again. "The last time I tried to kiss a girl, she fell into a lake."

"So? That girl moved on. *You* need a fresh start." Grandpa squeezed his shoulder. "All right, heart-to-heart over. Go hit the shower. You have a girl to woo."

The memory of Cara coming up from the water, spluttering curses, was too much to take, so he joked it away. "Woo? Who even says that anymore?"

Grandpa glared at him. "You can impress her. Take it a step at a time."

He rolled his eyes. "We'll see."

The Charger's engine always growled before he cut the ignition, and a curtain cracked open at the front of Faith's house. No turning back now—they knew he was here. Kyle pulled his cell phone from his pocket. One text: *All set. South door open. Casey knows you're coming.*

Good. His surprise was still in the works. Rolling his shoulders to relieve a little of the tension keeping them bunched around his ears, he climbed out of the car and headed to the front porch. Proof that someone had been watching, Mr. Gladwell opened the door two seconds after Kyle's knock.

He stood there staring Kyle down for a second. Behind him, on the dining room table, was the most beautiful bow Kyle had ever seen. Blood red fiberglass, obviously expensive, and in perfect fighting shape. A fletching kit for making arrows was laid out next to it. That couldn't be a coincidence.

Olympic archer. Right. "Hello, sir. Could I…um, is Faith here?"

Mr. Gladwell's eyebrow inched up, and he crossed his arms. "Yes, but only if you answer two questions."

Oh, shit. He was nervous enough, for God's sake. "Okay."

"One, you'll have my daughter home by curfew, correct?"

"Yes, sir."

"Two, you won't take her anywhere dangerous, correct?"

"Correct. It's just dinner, sir."

The man's face relaxed into a smile. "I have to do that with every kid my girls date. If they give me attitude, I know they're no good."

"So, uh, I passed?"

"Kyle, you called me 'sir.' You definitely passed. Come on in."

His heart thundered in his chest like he'd run for third on a long drive to the corner of right field, praying he wouldn't get thrown out. Faith's dad was acting completely normal now, like nothing had happened. This man had one sick sense of humor.

"Hi, Kyle." Mrs. Gladwell glided into the room and gave his arm a squeeze. "The yard is looking lovely."

He managed a laugh. "Even with the grass pulled up?"

"Especially with the grass pulled up. I'm really pleased."

"Thanks."

Mrs. Gladwell didn't acknowledge him. She was staring at the dining room table with her eyes narrowed. "Gavin, please tell me you didn't do the thing where you try to put the fear of God into Faith's date by making arrows at my dining room table again."

"I'm not putting the fear of God into anyone," Mr. Gladwell said, smirking. "I'm putting the fear of *meeting* God into these boys."

A flush climbed Kyle's neck and flooded his face with heat. Sweat prickled on his nose. "Should I, uh, say my prayers, sir?"

Mr. Gladwell burst out laughing. "Okay, I like this one. Much better than the other kid."

"His name was Cameron," Mrs. Gladwell said, shooting a sidelong look at Kyle. "And we probably shouldn't be discussing him."

"Good, because that kid was a punk," Mr. Gladwell muttered before he waved and disappeared into the living room."

Mrs. Gladwell shook her head, smiling. "You'll have to forgive him. Raising three girls makes for an overprotective—and warped—father."

Kyle nodded, relieved the conversation was over and wondering where he should put his hands. Behind his back? Clasped in front? Folded in prayer that Faith would come down soon, before he had to make small talk? Which was so stupid, because he did business with her mom. He had no trouble talking about plants, but now that they were "the parents," standing here with either of them, shooting the breeze, was pure torture.

"Sorry I'm late!"

Faith came in, and Kyle's heart stopped. She'd let her hair down, instead of pulled back in a bun, and her mile-long legs were on full display in a pair of skinny jeans. Her cheeks were slightly pink, but she looked happier and more chill than he'd seen since he met her. He was doing the right thing, asking her out, so he should probably chill, too.

He must've been staring, because Mrs. Gladwell stifled a laugh and said, "You kids have fun."

Smiling, she left for the living room, too. Now they were alone. Kyle couldn't think of a word to say. Faith was looking him up and down, smiling.

A few more seconds passed before Mr. Gladwell called, "You two going or do you want to stay here and play Yahtzee?"

They laughed. "We're leaving, Dad," Faith called back. "Geez, whoever heard of a father kicking her daughter out on a date."

And with that, they stepped out onto her front porch. She shut the door behind them, then turned to face him. "So, now what?"

He smiled slowly, finally feeling his confidence return. "It's still a surprise."

Chapter Twenty

FAITH

They started down the sidewalk, and Faith couldn't believe her legs still worked. God, Kyle looked nice. She'd been surprised by the khaki shorts and Polo yesterday, but today he wore a pair of jeans that fit him in all the right places, along with an untucked button-down. He turned to check if she was following and she had to snap her gaze back to his face. The corner of his mouth turned up, then he swaggered to the car, probably overdoing it just for her.

Her cheeks grew warmer. *No, Kyle, I'm not staring at your ass. You have a piece of lint stuck there. Can I pull it off for you?*

Oh, Lord.

"So, we're taking the Charger tonight?" she asked to fill the void of awkward silence threatening to make her run back to the safety of her house. Why was it so easy to flirt with him, to lean in, when they were in the backyard, but she felt so stiff and unsure now?

"I, uh, thought you might like it better." Kyle opened her door, but his expression…he looked uncertain, too. "Did you want to ride in the truck instead?"

She shook her head quickly. "No, the Charger's great. I've always wanted to see what one was like, aside from being fast."

He visibly relaxed. "They are, but I promise not to drive like an idiot tonight."

It took him longer than it should have to come around the car after closing her door. In her side-view mirror, she caught him pausing to take a deep breath, his shoulders drawing back and his chest expanding out.

When he got into the driver's seat, she asked, "Are you okay?"

"What? Oh, I'm fine." He flashed her his typical "I own the world" smile. "But…are you scared to ride in this car with me? Because I promised your dad I'd drive safe."

She couldn't help but melt a little inside. He'd actually paid attention to her dad? Cameron had spent more time mocking her parents' overprotective nature after the fact than listening. "I'm not scared at all." She leaned back in her seat. The leather was supple as a well-worn pair of jeans. "This is one sexy car, though."

Kyle raised an eyebrow and turned the key in the ignition. The engine rumbled to life, vibrating the entire car. "You have no idea."

She laughed and her hand flew to her mouth. He reached out and pulled it away. "Why do you put your hand over your mouth when you laugh?"

She swallowed her laughter and cocked her head. "I do?"

"Yes, you do." He smiled, puzzled. "It's cute, but I like it when you smile, so…"

He nodded at her wrist in his hand, and a little shiver ran through her middle. "I never noticed, I guess. I don't know why I do it."

He leaned across the console between them, eyes alight. "I'll help you quit the habit if you want me to. Means some hand-holding, though. Any objections?"

Her heart stuttered over a few beats. "No." She stared down at his hand and wriggled her wrist until her hand was in his. "Cameron thought holding hands was childish. But he's a douche."

He gave her a solemn nod. "He is."

She met his gaze, feeling something unwind inside her. "And you're not."

Kyle stared down at the console. "You don't know me, Faith."

"Not much. Not yet," she answered softly. "But I like what I see so far."

He cleared his throat and let go of her hand. She wasn't sure if she should be hurt by that or not, but when he turned to check his side-view mirror, she noticed a grin spreading across his face.

He put the car in gear, both hands on the wheel—which made her feel better about him letting go—and they glided away from the house. The Charger growled its way through town although, true to his word, Kyle stuck to the speed limit. Okay, maybe five miles an hour over, but that didn't really count.

Faith peered out the window. The sun had long since retired and streetlights glowed as they drove to downtown, where historic buildings and trendy restaurants lined the sides of the road. "Will you tell me where we're going?"

"I will," he answered, flipping on the right turn signal. "Because we're here."

He pulled into the lot at the Suttonville Gardens and Arboretum. There wasn't a single car around, and all the lights were off, save a few in the back of the large greenhouse that held most of the exhibits. A little knot of anxiety burrowed into her spine. Just what did he think was going to happen here?

"Um, I think they're closed," she squeaked, instantly hating herself for sounding so timid. *Seize the day, girl!* That thought was in Vi's voice, but it wasn't any less true.

Kyle was watching her. "I know the manager. He said we could tour the gardens after hours, a private showing. If you'd rather go somewhere else, we could—"

He sounded so earnest, not like a guy trying to seduce a naive dancer. And it was *the arboretum*. He'd brought her to a place that meant something to him. Not some party, cheesy club, or even to his house for his version of "Netflix and chill." He'd brought her to a place full of plants, and from his expression, he really wanted her to like it.

She unfroze and smiled. "There's no other place I'd rather be."

His smile in return was pleased. "Good. Because the place isn't the only surprise. Come on, I'll show you."

Deciding to trust in whatever Kyle had cooked up, she climbed out of the car. "Lead the way."

They entered the greenhouse through a back door. Kyle had a key. "Where'd you get that?"

"I know a guy," he said, sounding a lot more sure of himself now. "I think you'll enjoy it."

They went through a tiny office and a nursery of sorts, where little trees were propped up in posts with sticks and twine. "This is where they start seedlings," he said, pointing at one group of pots. The trees were barely eight inches high. "Those are from a historic pecan in the park. They're trying to replicate it."

He went to a small fridge in the corner that she hadn't noticed and pulled a shopping bag out. She frowned. "We're not here to steal plants, are we?"

He laughed, and it changed his whole face. He looked younger, vulnerable. "I promised you dinner, remember?"

She stared down at her shoes. When would she ever figure out how to talk to him? Probably right after they graduated and she never saw him again. "Right."

He came over and took her hand. It was warm in hers, and she realized she'd been missing it since he let go in the car. "Now for the surprise."

She followed him into the main greenhouse, warm and humid after the cool spring night. Exotic plants bloomed everywhere she looked, a riot of pinks, reds, oranges, and purples. The air hung heavy with the scent of earth and green things growing. Faith took a deep breath. Underneath the smell of gardening soil, a dozen different perfumes tickled her nose.

"Wow," she whispered.

"You've never been here, have you?" Kyle's eyes sparkled, and he seemed pleased by her reaction.

"No. I missed the field trip in third grade." She turned, taking it all in. "It's beautiful."

"This isn't even the best part." He squeezed her hand, and heat climbed the back of her neck. "Over here."

"Over here" turned out to be a small lawn lining a huge bed of azaleas in spring colors of pink, lavender, and white. A white blanket was spread out on the grass next to a picnic basket.

A whole host of butterflies took flight in her stomach. "How did you do all this?"

"Like I said, I know a guy." Kyle's cocky smile was back. "Well, more than one."

Faith sank down on the blanket and crossed her legs, wishing, for once, that they weren't so long. She wasn't used to being self-conscious, but something about Kyle made it all too easy. Like it was important to impress him, and wondering if she was good enough. "I love it."

He set the bag down and knelt to dig through it. "Good." The look he shot her was intense. "You deserve to have someone try to impress you."

She ducked her head, not sure what to think, having just wondered how to impress *him*. Seems like they were both trying too hard. "Not more than any other girl."

"True. Most girls deserve it, but it never happens." His voice was soft. "Which is why it's your turn."

"With you?" she asked, teasing. "Why, Kyle, I'm shocked."

He flushed. "That's, um, not exactly what I meant."

"It's okay. I know you've dated a lot of girls. And I *am* impressed." She reached out to brush a pink azalea petal with her fingertip, not sure what to think. Was she really special to him, or was this his way of pulling her into the Kyle Sawyer Mile-High Club? "But you don't have to make this kind of effort just for my sake. I know what the score is."

He turned away, unpacking little sandwiches, strawberries, and cookies from the bag. "And what's the score?"

She took a deep breath. This *felt* like a date, but she needed to know before she let herself believe it. "That we're in this scheme together. You don't have to pretend to be my boyfriend except when we need to put on a show. Isn't that what this is?" There, she'd said it. She wished she could take it back.

But she really wanted an answer

Chapter Twenty-One

KYLE

Faith's question felt like a fastball to the chest—crushing and knocking the wind out of him. He was trying so hard, and she thought he was playing a game? God, he just couldn't win. But he'd promised himself—and Grandpa—that he'd stick with it, and for once, he would.

"I brought you here because I thought you'd like it," he said quietly, trying to force the confusion out of his voice. "You've helped me work on the backyard and I wanted to say thank you."

There, that sounded neutral, right? Not *Faith, you're the nicest girl I've met, and I want to kiss you for nine hours straight.* Now that? That sounded desperate.

Faith's eyebrow raised. "Is that all?"

Damn, she called his bluff fast. "What else do you want it to be?"

She leaned back and turned her head toward the flowers. "I don't know. Not exactly."

He resumed unpacking their picnic, trying not to get his hopes up too far. "Neither do I. So I think maybe we should try to be friends, or whatever, just to see."

She faced him, and her cheeks were as pink as the Autumn Carnival azaleas behind her. "I'd like that. I could use a good friend right now."

"Me, too."

She nodded briskly. "So, dinner?"

"Dinner."

They ate mostly in silence, but he could tell that Faith was slowly thawing out. She kept looking around at all the plants. "So do you know what most of these are?" she finally asked.

"I know what all of them are," he said, willing her to look at him. "I volunteer here." He paused. "Please don't tell anyone that."

"Why not?"

His mouth opened and closed. She had no idea he wasn't exactly what she assumed, and he'd as much as announced it. "It's, um…people can be jerks about guys who like to work on yards."

"And you have a reputation to protect."

Her tone was far too knowing for comfort. Did she suspect? "Something like that. Anyway, what about you? I know you dance."

"And I sing." Her hands settled in her lap.

"Are you going to keep doing it after we graduate?"

"I hope so." She shrugged, but he could tell it cost her to act like she didn't care. "I applied to NYU. They have a great musical theater program. I'm waiting to hear back."

He nodded, trying not to make a big deal out of it, since she didn't seem to want to. Still, she must be crazy talented to even think about applying. "Good luck. And what about the musical at school?"

She laughed. "You know about that?"

"Fliers. At school." Thank God Vi had given him an out here. "You're Laurey?"

Faith's eyes lit up. "I'm surprised you'd know that, but yes. And it's the best role ever."

She chattered about the costumes, the music, and the story for a good ten minutes, before stopping abruptly. Talking about the performance made her light up. Her eyes were sparkling and she gestured around, pretending to point out things about the set. She looked kind of like he felt when he talked to the head horticulturalist at the arboretum: joyful. The theater was her garden, and he leaned in, listening. If this is what made her happy, he wanted to know about it.

Abruptly, she stopped, her cheeks pink. "Sorry. I kind of ran on there."

"I like listening to you," he said, before thinking.

She bit her lower lip. "No guy's ever said that to me before."

Kyle let out a breath he didn't know he'd been holding. "I'm not like other guys."

"No, you're not," she said, toying with a few loose azalea petals.

"Is that…a bad thing?" he asked.

"No." Faith gave him a brief smile. "That's not what I'm worrying about. I was just thinking about part of the musical. There could be a problem."

He scooted forward and touched her knee. When she didn't flinch or move away, he left his hand there. "What?"

"It's silly…but there's a lift in the ballet scene and my partner hasn't bothered to practice with me yet. I'm not sure if I can hold the pose. I'm worried I'll end up overshooting and toppling us both over."

Was that all? He gave her a quick, clinical looking-over— or so he tried to tell himself it was clinical and not outright ogling. She probably weighed a buck twenty-five. That was nothing. He hauled fifty pound bags of mulch, two at a time, all day. Surely her partner could lift her, but if she was worried about her part, how hard could it be to help her out?

Kyle pushed himself to his feet and held out a hand to help her up. "Show me."

Now her cheeks went scarlet. "Oh, no, you don't have to…"

"If it's bugging you, I want to help." He gave her a quick once-over, and she ducked her head. The shyness was cute. "Tell me what to do."

She took a deep breath, then stepped in close and turned her back on him. He barely breathed as she reached for his hands and placed them on her hips. "On the count of three, I'm going to jump, and you're going to lift me to chest level. Turn in a slow circle, then bring me down."

"Sounds easy." Crap, did she hear his voice shake just then? "Let's do it."

She let out a surprised chuckle, but this time she didn't let her hand fly to her mouth. "Sorry. I have a problem with inappropriate laughter."

He grinned and leaned his head on her shoulder. "Not so inappropriate, given what I said. Now, you ready?"

"Yep." She stood up taller. "One…"

He tightened his hands on her hips, and he could've sworn she shivered. Her skin was warm through her jeans, and he knew he'd be sorry to let go.

"Two…"

Faith went up on her toes, the crown of her head reaching his forehead. Man, she was tall.

"Three!"

She dropped down suddenly, bending her knees outward, then she sprang up. He almost let go, surprised by the power of her vertical leap. She was so strong, he had to tighten his forearms and really hang on to keep from losing her. Between her momentum and the strength in his arms from baseball, he managed to lift her up so that her hips were level with his face.

Oh, holy shit. The view almost made him drop her.

It wasn't just that he was getting a very close, personal look, but the way she held her body, arms aloft, legs bent gracefully, back straight, made him skip a heartbeat or four. She was every bit as strong as any athlete he'd ever known, and ten times as graceful.

"Now turn!" Faith ordered.

Right, he needed to turn. He made it around, slowly, without dropping her, then lowered her to the ground. She came down balancing on her toes, despite wearing little canvas tennis shoes instead of ballet slippers, and spun in the circle of his arms to face him.

Grinning, she wrapped her arms around his neck. "That was perfect. Thank you."

Their faces were only inches apart, and their bodies were even closer. Her smile faded as her eyes drifted to his lips, then back to his eyes.

Holding on to his courage as tightly as he'd held her during the lift, he leaned in, moving slow in case she decided this wasn't a good idea.

She didn't pull away.

He paused a breath away from her lips, uncertain. "I'd like to kiss you."

A little smile twitched at the corner of her mouth. "I kind of guessed that."

Okay, that was a yes, right? His insides rolled. God, if he messed this up, she'd know. Faith would figure out that this wasn't his nine-hundredth kiss.

It was his first.

When he didn't move, she closed the gap and pressed her lips to his. Surprised, he didn't shut his eyes right away, focusing on the tiny freckles on the bridge of her nose. Then his brain caught up with his body. He pulled her close, pressing the length of her against him, and let his eyes fall shut. Not wanting her to notice he hadn't done this before, he let her set the pace on the kiss, startling when she teased his lower lip with her tongue. Surely his heart would burst out of his chest any second. If it did, he'd let it, mainly because he knew it would run straight for Faith.

After what seemed like hours, she gently pulled away. "Did I forget to say it was okay to kiss me?"

He laughed, and it sounded low and gravelly. So *that* was what all the fuss was about. He'd need to sit down soon if his knees didn't stop shaking. "I liked your answer just fine."

A door slammed shut at the back of the arboretum. "Kyle? I need to close up."

"That must be your guy." She lowered her eyes, now shy. "Should we go?"

"Yeah." Even if he didn't want to. He'd kissed her—for real. And he wanted to do it again, but Casey was stacking pots loudly in the nursery, so he packed up the picnic instead, making sure all crumbs and traces were removed.

"You're being pretty thorough with cleanup. Should I help?" Faith asked.

Her voice was shaky, and that warmed him all the way through. He wasn't the only unsteady one. "It's okay. I just wanted to make sure we left the garden in good shape."

As they walked back to the nursery, Faith slipped her hand into his. "Thanks for dancing with me."

He smiled, his emotions running riot. How could someone be happy, turned on, scared, worried, and triumphant all at the same time? He hadn't been this mixed-up-elated since he caught the last out in the state championship last year, and the team rushed to dog-pile him.

He nudged Faith lightly with his hip. "Thanks for letting me."

Chapter Twenty-Two

Kyle was really quiet on the ride home. She didn't press him—there was too much to think about. Like how he smelled of starched cotton and sage. He'd been planting some that day—apparently Mom had asked to add an herb garden in the backyard.

The scent had her all kinds of distracted. But it was crazy, right? She still didn't have a good read on him. So far, she saw no hint of the scary, delinquent boy she'd heard about. He had a sweet side, almost shy. If she hadn't known better, she would've guessed she was his first kiss. He seemed so unsure about it, and eager, too, once she made the decision for him.

She bit back a chuckle. He was a better actor than she was, turned out. *Kyle Sawyer's first kiss. As if.*

Still, she'd enjoyed the sweetness of it. Cameron's first kiss had been aggressive. He'd smashed his mouth to hers like they were in a movie where the heroes had just saved the world. She'd taught him to back off a bit, but the emotion behind it wasn't the same.

She glanced at Kyle's profile. He was staring at the road with intense concentration, like the center lines were going to morph into a pack of dragons and chase them down the street. It wasn't so much that he was ignoring her. It was more like he was trying to pretend he was, because when she looked at him, his hands tightened on the steering wheel.

They pulled up in front of her house twenty minutes before curfew. As expected, lights blazed out of the living-room window, and the porch light was on full blast. Dad's silhouette was outlined in the sheer curtains. He was sitting in his chair, probably pretending to read, but really waiting to see how long it was before she left the car and opened the door. The lights, per usual, were to discourage any good-night kiss activity. Faith loved her parents, but the freedom of living in New York sounded really appealing right now.

"I, um, probably better go up." She touched Kyle's arm, and he jumped. "Oh, sorry. You okay?"

His typical cocky smile showed up. "Yeah, sure. Thanks for coming out with me tonight."

She bit back a frown. He looked shaken, rather than sure of himself. "Are we still on for the charade at Dolly's?"

"I am if you are." Now his expression looked more natural—and a tiny bit concerned. "You're absolutely sure about this? Today it's just a rumor. Tomorrow the genie is out of the bottle for good."

She straightened her spine and looked him right in the eye. "Yes. I'm completely sure. See you in the morning?"

"Sure." He started to lean across like he was going to kiss her again, then paused, before finally planting a quick peck on her cheek. "See you then."

And that was all. Disappointment came over her all at once. Every time she thought they were getting closer he shut down, leaving her out in the cold.

Kyle came around to open her door and walked her halfway up to her house. "Faith…"

She stopped and turned to face him. "Yes?"

He opened his mouth, then closed it. "Nothing. Just… you're going to do great at the musical."

Her stomach swooped. And there he was again, back from wherever he seemed to disappear. "You haven't even heard me sing."

"I don't need to." He headed back to the Charger. "I know."

Stunned, she watched him climb into his car and start it. He didn't leave, though. Oh, right. He was waiting for her to go inside safely, despite the fact that her dad was now *standing* in the living room window. She waved and turned up the sidewalk.

Her dad opened the door before she fished her key out of her purse. "Have a nice time, pumpkin?"

"Dad, I'm eighteen. Don't you think I'm a little old for 'pumpkin' now?"

"You'll be sixty and I'll be in a home, and I'll still call you pumpkin. Now, let's move the subject back to your date with our gardener."

"One, he's not our gardener. Two, yes, I had fun. He took me to the arboretum."

"Huh." Dad scratched his head. "Based on the car alone, I was worried I'd have to come up with bail after a wild night of clubbing."

"You'd think," Faith murmured. "He wanted to show me their azalea display. He knows I like them."

"I should think so, considering the eight bushes in the backyard." Dad smiled, and the wrinkles around his eyes deepened. "You look happy, and that's what counts. After half your dates with that Cameron kid, you looked like you wanted to strangle something—preferably him."

"It did kind of get that way, didn't it? I'm glad I moved on." She gave Dad a brief hug. "I'm going upstairs."

He nodded and returned to his chair. Maybe to make her think he wasn't up to watch for her. They'd done this enough, though, that she knew better. He was silly, but he cared. That was more than could be said for some of her friends' dads.

She flopped down on her bed, reliving that kiss. He'd been more hesitant than she expected, like he wanted to let her have control so she wouldn't back away. And taking her to see azaleas for a date? Everything about tonight had been about *her*. Even the way he hopped up, asking to help her with the lift, so serious about giving it a try. She'd never wanted to kiss a guy more than in that moment. It was perfect.

Almost.

She just needed to figure out what was bothering him. He was holding something back, and she wanted to know what—and why.

Her phone buzzed in her purse. Of course it was Violet, texting one minute after curfew because she knew Faith would be home.

V: *So, how's things?*

Faith laughed. *Oh, you know. Just sitting at home watching the clock hands move.*

V: *Don't make me come over there.*

F: *Okay, okay. The date was very nice. He was very nice. The kiss was very nice.*

V: *KISS?!!!! Is there more?*

F: *Just the kiss—he's so much sweeter than I thought*

he'd be.

V: *What, no groping? Pshaw. He's not living up to my expectations.*

F: *Maybe not…but he's been way above mine.*

V: *Girl, after Cameron, you have NO expectations. What about tmo?*

F: *We're still on. He'll drive me up there around six.*

V: *Good. I have confirmation there will be a good crowd. Maybe even Cam.*

Faith's stomach dropped. For all her confidence with Kyle, she still wasn't sure how she'd do this. *What, did you tell everyone to be there?*

V: *Mayyybeeee*

F: *Vi! Guh, okay. Yes, we'll be there.*

And hopefully, put on a show no one would forget.

Chapter Twenty-Three

When Kyle came in from the garage, Grandpa was waiting for him at the kitchen table, the remnants of a piece of chocolate cake on a plate in front of him. He had on plaid PJs and a ratty robe Grandma had bought for him fifteen years ago.

"Is there more of that?" he asked, and Grandpa pointed to the counter. Rosanna must've baked them one before leaving. He cut himself a slice, grimacing when his hands shook on the knife.

"How'd it go, kid?"

Right to the heart of things. That was the old man's style. "Well. She liked the flowers."

"And?"

He rolled his eyes. "I kissed her."

"Yeah, you did!" Grandpa grinned, slapping a wrinkled hand against the tabletop. "Get over here and sit so I can grill you."

Kyle told the story as simply as he could, trying to stay

calm about it. Faith treated him so differently than other girls. She was funny and quick, and didn't seem to care about any of the stories. Instead, she looked right through him, like she knew exactly what he was thinking.

Like she knew exactly who he was.

"She sounds like a lovely girl." Grandpa wiped chocolate from his mouth with a napkin. "I'm proud of you, boy. You seeing her again?"

"Tomorrow."

"That sounds good. Did the trick about getting her to talk about the musical work?"

Kyle nodded, and the muscles in his arms tensed, almost like he was about to lift her again. "She appreciated that. I have the feeling her d-bag ex never talked about anything but himself."

"Great." Grandpa stood. "I'm off to bed. Keep it up, Kyle. Be yourself, and everything will work out."

Be himself. It sounded so easy, except he wasn't sure who he was. Faith had already seen more of the "real" him than anyone. But would she continue to like what she saw? "I'll try."

Grandpa shuffled out of the kitchen, leaving Kyle to pick at his cake. That roiling mix of emotions from earlier hadn't subsided much. The more he saw of Faith, the more he wanted their time together to be real, and not part of "the plan." She seemed interested, so maybe he should keep going in this direction, see how it went.

A tiny voice in the back of his head whispered awful things, how he wasn't good enough. How he was a fraud and a liar. How a girl like Faith could never like a guy like him. Those thoughts had pelted him the whole way home, guilt for letting his need to kiss her outweigh the need to keep her at arm's length so she wouldn't be hurt. When she'd asked if he was okay, he'd almost snapped before realizing it.

He stood suddenly, his chair scraping against the hardwood floor, cake forgotten. He wasn't going to listen to that doubting voice, not tonight. No matter what fears he had, no matter what humiliations lurked in his past, he was going to *try* with this girl. And to hell with anyone — or any voice — who told him otherwise.

Because if he knew anything at all, the way Faith looked at him tonight was enough to chase away doubt.

The next morning, after stopping by the nursery for sod, Kyle prodded the Toyota over to the Gladwells'. Faith's Bug was in the driveway, but the other cars were gone. So she was here alone. He bit back a smile. Maybe it was time to test his resolve — and hers.

He glanced at the sod in the bed of the truck. It was already humid and unseasonably warm out again today. Whistling like everything was normal, just in case Faith was watching him from the house, he unloaded the sod and carted it to the backyard. A flicker of movement in the blinds upstairs caught his eye. Good, he was hoping for an audience.

Kyle made a big show of wiping his forehead and pulled his T-shirt over his head. After tossing it onto the porch steps, he stretched his arms high over his head. Something thumped against the window upstairs, and he choked on a laugh as he squatted to pick up a roll of sod, making sure to use every muscle in his arms, back, and shoulders to do the job.

The door from the house to the porch creaked open, but he pretended he hadn't heard it. Still whistling, he went about laying out rolls of new grass onto the plot under the large oak tree. He bent and flexed every chance he had, methodically working as if the girl he was hoping to drive crazy wasn't sneaking a very long peek, hiding behind the sofa on the porch.

He whistled louder. His cheeks were starting to hurt, but he wanted to make sure she heard him. Still nothing except his knowledge she was watching. He just had to try harder, then.

He stood, went to his water thermos, and steeled himself before dumping some water over his head so that it ran down his back and chest. A little squeak, then a sound like hands being clapped over a mouth, came from the porch.

Okay, game over. He walked into a patch of sunlight and stared straight at her hiding place, knowing full well water was dripping down his torso. He whistled his tune one more time.

This time, Faith's head popped up over the back of the couch, eyes gleaming. "That was some show. Have you seen *Oklahoma!*?"

He whistled the chorus to "People Will Say We're in Love" again. "I heard a girl I like is playing Laurey. I wanted to check it out."

Even from here, even with him in sun, and her in shadow, he could tell her cheeks were turning pink. "That was nice of you," she said. "Are you planning to be shirtless all day today? Because if you are, I thought I'd invite Vi over for some popcorn and to watch you work."

He laughed. "If Violet comes over, I'm afraid I'll have to put it back on. I prefer to show off in private."

"Do you now." Faith came to the door leading outside, but didn't open it. She raised an arm over her head and leaned against the doorjamb, her long, lean body on full display in a pair of athletic shorts, a tank, and a hoodie.

Now who was playing whom?

He took a few steps toward the porch, a pull dragging him closer to her. "I'm thoughtful like that."

Her smile turned slightly teasing, and his pulse kicked up. "Do you give private audiences to all your girls?"

The truth almost strangled him, but he shoved it away. Confidence. That was today's word. "Just one."

He watched as the smile fell from her face, replaced by something cute, embarrassed, shy. She dropped the sultry pose and wrapped her arms around her middle. "Oh. Um, then I suppose I should say thank you for giving me the exclusive performance?"

He climbed the porch steps and stood in front of her, the screen door the only thing between them. He pressed a hand against the screen. "Or you could say you enjoyed it."

She started to cover her mouth, laughing, but pulled it away. "Oh, I think that's a given." She rested her hand against his, warm despite the screen. "How much work do you need to do today?"

He glanced over his shoulder. The truth was he only had a few more hours now that everything was in place. He thought about dragging it out so he could come back tomorrow, but maybe he would need that excuse to see her. "I'm almost done, but I have practice at two, so I'll have to finish tomorrow."

"But you don't have to leave until, what, one thirty?" When he nodded, she smiled and backed away from the door. "Then I'll see you at noon for lunch. Shirt optional."

It took a lot of effort not to pump a fist to the sky once she disappeared into the house. He raced into the yard and hurried to finish laying the sod. Whatever she had planned, there was no way he'd make her wait.

Nerves be damned.

Chapter Twenty-Four

Faith leaned against the kitchen counter, hands over her face. Her cheeks were hot to the touch and she laughed so hard, she had to wheeze to draw breath. Kyle watched *Oklahoma!* for her? That was hard enough to believe, but she could get used to the whole shirtless-lawn-guy thing.

Maybe Vi was right—maybe it was time to let go and enjoy herself. Kyle would most certainly be a good time, and the more she saw of him—which was a lot—the more she found herself wanting something more. Whatever had come up between them probably wouldn't last forever, but forever was a long time, and right now sounded pretty good.

She flew upstairs to take a shower and throw on nicer shorts, then ran back downstairs to make lunch. He'd surprised her with dinner. She'd return the favor and see what happened. Her parents would be gone all day. Plenty of time to cook up some trouble.

At exactly noon, Kyle knocked at the back door. He

knocked. God, he could be really adorable sometimes. She drifted across the porch and faced him through the screen. His hair was damp, but his shirt was on. His hands were clean, too. He caught her looking. "I borrowed the hose. I didn't want to come inside wearing most of the backyard."

"I wouldn't have cared, but thanks." She took a deep breath and opened the door. "I made us some lunch. It's just sandwiches…"

"That sounds great."

Despite all the flirting earlier, Faith's middle fluttered with nerves. She wasn't sure where she was going with all this, but if they were going to put on a show at Dolly's, they probably should give the whole kissing thing another try beforehand. "Um, you want something to drink? We have lemonade."

Kyle took a seat at the table. "Yes, please."

"You, uh, ready for this afternoon?" she asked. "Cameron might be there."

Kyle's shoulders hunched briefly, then they relaxed, but it looked forced. "That's good, right?"

Faith put her sandwich down. "Kyle, can I ask you something?"

He set his down, too, looking worried. "Of course."

"What's the problem with you and Cameron? You know my reasons. Before I…" She swallowed and made herself go on. "Before *we* make out in front of everybody. I'm trusting you with a lot."

"Faith, I'm trusting you, too." He met her gaze. "You're right, though, you have a right to know." He paused. "You ever been bullied? Not just the petty stuff, but bad enough to wish you could leave town? To…"

Faith heard what he didn't say. She put her hand on his arm. "You don't have to tell me."

"I do." He flexed his hand, and his arm muscles tightened in her grip. "Cameron has a set of friends. A pack of four."

She nodded. "Cam, Jake, Braden, and Andrew."

"Right." He was staring at a point beyond her shoulder. "Those four made my life miserable, and they roped a lot of people into it. Most of it was stupid bullshit—tripping me in the hall, whispering crap behind my back. Stealing my homework. I told you I'm dyslexic, right?"

"Yes."

"Okay, so it takes *hours* to do my homework, and I was making Ds in science in the spring of my seventh-grade year. Some of Cameron's friends were in my class and caught sight of one of my tests. I misspelled every other word, reversed stuff, and missed most of the multiple-choice stuff because I couldn't read the questions right. Anyway, they told Cameron, and he broke into my locker.

"I couldn't find my binder anywhere. All my homework, all the stuff Grandpa had notated for me, all my tests—gone. Next day, my graded work was taped up all over the school. All those Ds. Worse, those assholes had highlighted all the places where I spelled mammal 'lamal' and shit like that. I started tearing it down, but the damage was done. For the rest of seventh grade, I was the class idiot."

Faith blinked, unsurprised when an angry tear ran down her cheek. "I knew he could be petty, but that's outright cruel. I should slap his face."

But Kyle was shaking his head. "Don't. I can fight my own battles now, and I'd rather not have all that come up again. Most people have forgotten about it, even if I can't."

It seemed so unfair, though. Still, awful as that prank had been, Kyle's anger ran deeper than what she'd expect. She could tell there was more to the story, but she wouldn't pry. If he wanted to tell her everything, she could wait until he was ready. "I'm sorry it happened. And I'm glad we're doing this. Cameron deserves to be shown up."

He gave her a tight smile. "Maybe a little."

They sat in awkward silence, but she wasn't sure what to say. She wanted to lighten the mood, to drag Kyle out of the memories she could see were eating him alive. She wanted to make him forget Cameron and focus on her.

Which led to her blurting out, "Want to watch me dance?"

That earned her a soft smile that evaporated all the awkward the kitchen could hold. "I'd like that."

She clenched her hands in her lap to keep them from trembling. Why did she suggest that? Dancing in a production was one thing. Dancing for one guy, alone together? That was a whole other thing. A thing her parents might have a completely different word for: inappropriate.

Then again, maybe a little inappropriate was exactly what she needed.

"You don't have to, you know." Kyle's voice was kind. "I wasn't suggesting a talent show when I roamed the yard half naked. That was just to get your attention."

She nodded, flushing. "It worked. But no, I'd like to." And suddenly, she really did. "Go to the porch. I need to change and grab my shoes."

Plus going upstairs would give her a moment to breathe, which she most definitely needed to do. Once upstairs, she picked out a plain black leotard, a pink dance skirt, and tights. If she was going to do this, she had to do it right. Hair up in a bun, lip gloss, and all. And if her hands shook while tying her pointe shoes, so be it.

When she found him on the porch, he was sitting in one of the chairs across from the barre—and had moved all the other furniture against the walls. "How did you know?"

"About the furniture? I thought you might need room."

This guy was trying to steal her heart, wasn't he? He was doing a damn good job of it, too. Trembling all over, she went to the stereo, plugged in her phone. She found Tchaikovsky's Fifth, the second movement, and scrolled to the last three minutes. "This is something we did for recital last fall."

She didn't tell him she'd been the prima of the company. That didn't seem to matter much, not with the way he watched her as she took her place, standing in fourth position until the section of the piece she wanted started.

Relevé, arms up, turn. Madame's voice in her head, "Float, Faith. Like a flower petal."

And she did. The music poured through her, lifting her up. The Tchaikovsky was both powerful and delicate, making her feel strong, light. Balanced. All the sadness from the kitchen, the anger, the confusion, disappeared. In its place, she let all the happiness and contentment dancing could give settle into her bones.

After all her hours of practice, the moves were instinctive, and she forgot Kyle was there. Her mind was occupied with controlling her limbs, moderating her breathing, and ignoring the pain that came with each *relevé*, but that wasn't important. Only the dance was. She moved through it, letting the joy pulse in her veins.

The music hit its crescendo, and she spun, before landing in her final position, arms extended and chest heaving.

Then she remembered she had an audience.

Kyle was staring at her, his eyes dark and intense. Nothing mocking, nothing cocky. "That was beautiful, Faith."

She dropped her pose and stared at her pointe shoes. "Thank you."

The chair creaked, and she watched his feet close the distance between them as the third movement of the Tchaikovsky began. He put a finger under chin and tilted her face up to his. "I mean it. You have a lot of talent. NYU would be stupid not to let you in."

"And yet," she said in a shaking voice, "you still haven't heard me sing."

He smiled. "Sing our song, and I'll whistle along."

She stared at him, still breathless. That song from *Oklahoma!*? Surely that's not what he meant. "Now I know you're teasing me."

"Not really." His hands slid down her arms and encircled her waist. "Maybe not at all."

"Oh." She cleared her throat. "I'm not sure I'm ready to sing." A fleeting look of disappointment crossed his face, and she said, "Not the song, just in general. I'm a little out of breath."

"How about dancing, then?" He started turning them in a slow circle. "That okay?"

"Always," she murmured.

His body was tight against hers, his thin T-shirt and her leotard concealing almost nothing between them. Goose bumps rose along her arms when he leaned in to press his forehead to hers.

"What are we doing, Kyle?" she asked, almost afraid to hear his answer if it was going to be "having a good time," or "just messing around." Because this didn't feel like just messing around. This felt too big for just a quick hookup.

"Dancing." He pulled away to look into her eyes. "Because it's your favorite thing to do."

Oh God. He had her now. All in, whole heart. Being hurt would be worth it if this wasn't meant to last. "It is. But, um…" She gulped down a breath. "I like kissing a lot, too."

Those must've been magic words, because before she could take another breath, his lips were pressed against hers. One hand circled her waist, and the other was busily pulling the pins out of her bun, so that her hair spilled down her back.

She ran her hands down his arms and up to rest on his chest. He was all hard planes and angles. He gasped and pressed closer, pushing her back against the barre, and she stumbled.

"Sorry. Sorry." He wouldn't meet her eye. "Did I hurt

you?"

She looked at him, astonished. He'd been so eager, and a little clumsy, not at all like a guy with a ton of moves. "I'm fine, but maybe we should take this party inside. Oh, and maybe I should lose the pointe shoes."

"I don't know. Ballet shoes are pretty hot."

Laughing, she took his hand and led him through the kitchen to the family room. "You won't say that when you see my awful feet."

"Won't change a thing."

"You've been warned, then." She pointed at the couch. "Have a seat. I won't bite."

"That's disappointing."

She bent to untie her shoes so he wouldn't see her blush for the nineteenth time that day. When she finished and stood, he was staring at her again, looking rapt simply by the act of untying her shoes. She dropped them on the floor and glided over the hardwoods in her tights. "Should I go change?"

"No."

That simple word was delivered with force. Hmm, someone liked ballerinas, didn't he? She slid onto the couch next to him. "How long until you have to leave for practice?"

"About an hour."

His voice was hoarse. This was it, then. Time to jump off the high dive. "Perfect."

Chapter Twenty-Five

KYLE

Faith settled in his lap, a warm weight that set all his nerves on fire. And those legs? Those amazing, beautiful, long legs that danced like an angel? He had access to run his hands along them from midthigh to ankle. Her muscles flexed under his touch.

"You're lovely," he whispered.

"Lovely?" she murmured against his neck, before planting a kiss on his jaw. "That's not a word I hear guys our age use often. Hot, maybe."

He traced a line down her calf with his index finger. "Should I have said hot, then?"

"Hell no." She peered up at him. Her cheeks were flushed pink, and her eyelashes fluttered at him. "I'm all for lovely."

"Good." He ran his other hand up her back and tangled it in the hair at the base of her neck. "I'm glad I met you. You're different."

"So are you."

"Hmm." He kissed her cheek, the line of her long neck, her collarbone. "Is that bad?"

"Let me repeat. Hell no." She put her hands under his jaw and tilted his head up to meet his eyes. "I'm glad I met you, too."

He shifted her closer and kissed her softly. She kissed him back with more force, and one of her hands drifted to the hem of his T-shirt. She didn't try to pull his shirt over his head, but instead skimmed her fingers along his stomach. He'd never really grasped the concept of feeling both hot and cold, but he did now, and his hands shook on her back.

She pulled away, giving him a slightly bemused look. "Are you ticklish?"

"Uh." Damn, his brain was in lockdown. "No?"

She shook her head, smiling. "That sounded unsure. Just to be safe, though…"

She pulled her hand out of his shirt, and he kind of hated himself for losing the thread. Faith didn't get up, though. All she did was slow it down, and he felt a swell of relief. Which was *stupid*. Here he was with a beautiful girl in his lap, and he was nervous.

Calm down, nerves. I want to enjoy this.

They clung together on the couch, kissing, cuddling, for about thirty minutes before Kyle caught a glint of light through the window. "I think someone's here?"

She popped off his lap like a shot. "Mom. Go outside and pretend to work." She grabbed her pointe shoes and shoved him toward the porch. "Go."

His brain was having a little trouble switching gears from girl-in-his-lap to manual-labor-outside, but he stumbled behind her. She was already in the chair, tying her shoes around her ankles. "Hurry!"

He pushed through the screen door as another door slammed inside the house. "Faith? Baby?"

Cutting it close. He jogged into the yard and knelt over some loose sod, tugging at it like he was putting it in place. A moment later he heard Mrs. Gladwell ask Faith how long she'd been practicing.

The porch door swung open. "Kyle, this looks amazing."

He smeared extra dirt on his hands to make it look good, then stood. "Thank you, ma'am. It's just about finished. I'll need to come by tomorrow and water it in, then reprogram your sprinkler system. Will it do for your party next week?"

"More than." Mrs. Gladwell nodded. "It's perfect."

He nodded, thankful his heart rate had slowed. "If it's all the same to you, I'm going to head out. I have baseball practice, and I promised to take Faith out for some ice cream afterward."

She beamed. "That's fine with me."

He caught Faith watching him over her mother's shoulder. She had one hand over her mouth, no doubt trying to hide a laugh. "I'll be back around six then."

Now that his initial flustering had passed, he couldn't wait to have Faith back in his arms—especially with Cameron to see it.

Tonight was going to be amazing. He could feel it.

"So, what's the story?" Tristan pointed his mitt at Kyle. "Word's out you aren't just seeing Cameron's ex, but exploring places no man's gone before. I need details."

"None of your business." Kyle brushed past him and jogged up the steps of the dugout.

"Aw, come on!" Tristan ran behind him on their way out to the outfield for fielding practice. "I live for your stories, man. You know it!"

Kyle focused on the grass under his feet. The field had

been mowed while they took a break, and the air smelled like cut grass with a faint hit of fresh chalk from the new lines. He took a deep breath, trying to forget the way Faith's hair felt in his fingers. He'd miss every catch coming his way if he thought about her. And Tristan wasn't helping.

"You texted me, asking about her." Tristan ran up and bumped him. "Why won't you tell me what's going down, asshat?"

Kyle sighed. When it was just a game, running his mouth had been part of it. Now telling Tristan anything seemed cheap. "We're going to Dolly's later. You wanna know? Be there. I heard Cameron might be there, so it wouldn't be a bad idea to have some backup."

Tristan raised his eyebrows. "I will. See if the rumors are true." He laughed. "Sometimes I wonder if you're not just full of shit. I mean, the stories are great, but it'll be nice to get some proof, you know?"

Kyle forced a smile, even though his insides were freezing. "Guess you'll have to wait and see. Now shut up and get into position. Coach is giving us a death stare."

Tristan saluted and jogged to center field, leaving Kyle to wonder if his house of cards would come crashing down, or if Faith would help keep his rep intact…without ever finding out.

Chapter Twenty-Six

As soon as her mom went to her room to change, Faith rushed upstairs and closed her bedroom door behind her. She slid down the door to sit on the floor, two fingers tracing her mouth. Her whole body tingled. Was this what it was like to fall for someone? The real thing? Her other three boyfriends—Cameron especially—hadn't made her feel so *seen*. So alive.

Kyle had told her she was lovely. How was it that a guy who supposedly ran through girls paid more attention than a guy who spent a year by her side? With Cameron, it was like he only wanted a girlfriend for the same reason guys wanted a hot car—to make himself look good. Kyle wasn't like that at all.

Tonight, everyone would know that she was over Cameron, and in the best way possible. She covered her face, hiding a grin. Not only was she getting Cam back for being a complete dick, her revenge was a crazy-wonderful guy. At some point she'd have to thank Cam for forcing her hand to break up with him.

Not yet, though. Oh, no, not yet.

She hopped up, twirled around her room to the closet and picked out her tightest T-shirt and skinny jeans. Hell hath no fury and all that. Oh, who was she kidding—the jeans were for Kyle, and his fascination with her legs.

She rushed through a shower and spent a long time straightening her hair. No buns, or braids, or ponytails tonight. Everything had to be perfect, and that meant the works, including makeup and something other than tennis shoes.

When the doorbell rang at six, she took one last look in the mirror, nodded, and bounded down the stairs. Kyle was standing next to her mom, but when he saw her, his eyes widened.

"What do you think?" she asked. "Good?"

He had to clear his throat before he answered. "Yeah. Perfect."

Mom turned her head so he wouldn't see the wry smile on her face, but Faith caught it. "You two be good. Don't stay out too late."

"We'll be back by nine," Kyle said, before Faith could answer.

"We'll be back before curfew." Faith raised her eyebrows at him. "But maybe by nine."

Mom coughed over a fit of laughter. Kyle's expression was that of a guy who'd been spun in a circle twenty times, then told to walk straight ahead.

"That's fine," Mom said. "Have fun."

Faith knew as soon as they left, Mom would laugh until she cried, so she might as well put her out of her misery. "We will. Bye."

She clasped Kyle's hand and dragged him outside. He didn't look like he could move on his own. "You okay?"

"Um, yeah. You look…different. Um…look, I'm sorry,

but all I can come up with is *damn.*"

She leaned against his side. "That'll do just fine."

"I was worried, you know, after the whole 'lovely' discussion, that it wouldn't be."

He was giving her a teasing smile, and she squeezed his arm. "Honestly, it's nice to be appreciated."

"More reason for us to go to Dolly's and show that ex of yours how this works."

Once they were on the road, Vi texted: *Cam's here with his bimbo. Time to shine, kids.*

"Vi says he's there." Faith's knee bounced. She halfway wanted to jump out of the car and run home. There really wasn't any turning back now, not after Violet spread the word, but she still felt like she'd swallowed live grasshoppers.

Kyle rested his free hand on her knee, stilling it. The warmth of his hand flooded her brain and calmed her nerves. "It'll be fine," he said in that slow, sure voice of his.

"Right, okay." Faith's shoulders relaxed. She hadn't noticed how tight they'd been. "Seriously, if all we have to do is make out a little in front of a crowd, that's not so bad, right?"

His hand tightened briefly on her knee, then he released it, but now *he* looked nervous. "Right."

They turned into Dolly's. The drive-in had been in Suttonville long before Sonic thought about coming to town, and most of the locals would go to Dolly's before they'd go anywhere else. During school breaks and on weekends, though, it turned into the informal high school hangout. Everyone would park, order shakes, and go car to car to visit friends. Now, if someone dumped some rum into a coconut cream shake, that was his business.

When the Charger glided into an empty spot—one next to Violet's car, which Vi had been standing in with her arms crossed, waving off anyone who wanted this prime real estate—every head turned.

Including Cam's.

Violet came to Faith's window. "Full audience. Curtain up."

Faith wiped her sweaty hands on her jeans. Kyle nodded. "You want some ice cream?"

She laughed. Ice cream seemed way too ordinary for this, and for some reason that steadied her nerves. "Chocolate shake, extra whipped cream."

He raised an eyebrow. "You like whipped cream?"

The way he said it turned her imagination on full blast. "Love it."

"Good to know." He ordered their shakes, then motioned for her to get out of the car. "You ready?"

She took a deep breath and tossed her hair. *I'm Laurey. I'm strong, and I can do anything.* "Yep."

They climbed out of the car at the same time and Kyle walked with measured steps around the hood to her side. Violet shot him a quick thumbs-up and vanished. He didn't seem to notice. His eyes were glued on Faith, looking her over slowly. Only a quick tilt of his chin indicated he was asking her, one more time, if she wanted to do this.

In answer, she smiled, grabbed hold of the belt loops of his jeans, and pulled him against her. He let out a surprised gasp when her mouth met his. They melted together, and Faith forgot all about the dozens of students watching, Cameron and Holly, and the carhops. Not even Violet's pleased, and very, very evil cackle made her want to stop.

Kyle's hand ran up her back. He pulled away to kiss her temple. "I'm saying something witty. Laugh."

Faith, drawing on her acting chops, let out a peal of laughter. Vi's delighted grin told her it was pretty convincing.

Then Kyle's mouth was back on hers. The shocked silence at the diner broke, and chatter slowly rose all around them. A few whistles. A few grumbles.

And best of all? Tristan yelling, "God damn it, Sawyer! I hate it when you're right."

Faith had no idea what that meant, but Kyle's mouth popped off hers. He turned a cheerful smile on the gaggle of baseball players across the patio and flipped off Tristan. They hooted and hollered. Tristan gave them a slow clap.

If she'd cared about her reputation at all right now, she would've blushed to the roots of her hair and dug a hole nine feet deep to hide in. Instead, she put her hands on Kyle's cheeks, turning him to face her again, and planted another kiss firmly on his lips.

This time Kyle let out a slightly frustrated growl. Yeah, maybe they were taking this a little too far for public.

But what if they were alone? Would she stop? Would she be able to hold out and ask herself if he was the right guy?

That was a very good question.

She pulled back and whispered so only he'd hear. "Looks like our ice cream is on the way out. We can probably quit showing off." Her lips brushed his ear. "Or not. It's up to you."

Chapter Twenty-Seven

Faith's cheeks were flushed, and from the way the hushed words tumbled from her mouth, this had nothing to do with being at Dolly's.

His palms went slick on her back, and his entire body went rigid. He really liked this girl, but he'd told so many lies. What would she think of him if she realized she'd just publicly made out with the only eighteen-year-old player *virgin* in all of Suttonville?

So much for destroying her reputation.

His lies had dug him into a trench he wasn't sure he could climb out of, no matter how much he wanted this girl. This sweet, kind, graceful girl, who watched him with shining eyes—she didn't deserve this. Not even a little.

"Kyle?" Faith tilted her head to get a better look at him. "You okay? Did I say something wrong?"

"Hey! Asshole!"

All his breath whooshed out in a gust. Irony was a bitch—

he'd just been saved by Cameron. He couldn't handle the guilt of pulling a fast one on Faith, but anger? Anger he could handle.

In fact, he was furious. With himself, to be honest, but Cameron would be an acceptable substitute. He was stomping their direction, flanked by five football players. Holly Masterson sat on the hood of Cameron's truck, looking hurt and scared.

Faith, on the other hand, was pushing to move around Kyle like she wanted to fight this fight. Not going to happen. He needed to hit something. Cameron's jaw, preferably. He couldn't be suspended for a fight outside of school, and this moment had been a long, long time in coming. He wasn't that eighth grader Cameron had punched in the face for standing up to him after one too many taunts. He could swing a bat and send a ball four hundred yards. Beating the hell out of Cameron would take less effort than that.

Kyle turned and held an arm out to keep Faith behind him. "Hey, Cam. How's it going?"

Cameron stood toe-to-toe with him. He was an inch shorter and twenty-five pounds lighter, at least, but like all bulldogs, he thought physics didn't matter. He poked Kyle in the chest. "What are you doing with my girl?"

"*Your* girl?" Kyle asked calmly, even though his fists were aching to pound this douche canoe. "I was under the impression that you cheated on her, and you two broke up. I didn't even meet her until the day after that, which means you aren't in the picture."

"Then how does it make you feel to have my leftovers? She's just using you to get back at me."

"How would *you* know?" Faith shouted. "It's not like we ever did it. It's not like that's a secret—you told the world. I never loved you, Cameron. You treated me like shit, then you talked trash about me all over school. Kyle is better to me than you ever could be. If I want to be with him, it's none of your business!"

Cameron lunged forward, and his football buddies sprang after him, trying to catch his arms, but he was too fast.

Kyle was faster. He caught Cameron's wrist in an iron grip and squeezed. In a dead voice, he said, "Stop. Now."

Cameron winced but didn't back down. "Or what? You're nothing but a big chickenshit. You know it and I know it. Don't forget—I owned you first."

It took all his self-control not to break Cameron's wrist. He let himself squeeze a little harder, though. "Past is past. And you know as well as I do that I could turn you inside out today. Let. It. Go."

The murmurs of the crowd around them swelled as the baseball team stalked over. "You heard him, jackass," Tristan said. "It's not a good idea to start something with a bunch of guys who carry baseball bats in their trunks—and know how to use them."

Cameron's face turned purple. "This isn't over."

"Go back to Holly," Faith said. "Leave us alone."

Cameron glared at her over Kyle's shoulder. "So that's how it's going to be? Your feelings are hurt, so you fight dirty? I knew you were going to break up with me before I even *started* up with Holly. I could tell. But you didn't bother to tell me, leaving me hanging for two months."

Faith stiffened, and Kyle pressed his back against her, to let her know he'd handle it. "You knew, and you still hung on? You waited until you could see the words 'I'm leaving you' stamped on her forehead, then cheated on her so you can say you broke up with her? Kind of pathetic, man."

"I'm not talking to you, Sawyer."

Faith huffed behind Kyle, and he pulled Cameron's arm up and back. "It's over whether you like it or not. Get over her and move on."

The manager of the drive-in came hustling out. "No fighting! You there—let the kid go!"

Kyle released Cameron's wrist. "We were just leaving. Good-bye, Cameron."

Staying in front of Faith, using the rest of his team to provide some cover, Kyle opened her car door and ushered her inside. The team hung around until he started the engine and backed out.

"Where to?" God, he was tired. The adrenaline from the fight was leaving him, and his legs shook whenever he tried to clutch or brake.

"Wherever." Faith sounded just as tired, and belatedly, he noticed the tears rolling down her cheeks.

"Hey, it's over now." He reached over to pat her knee. "All done."

"Do you think I hurt his feelings?"

Kyle's mouth dropped open. "You care if you did?"

"Well, yeah." She sniffled. "I'm such an idiot. I'm sorry, Kyle. I pushed things too far, didn't I? He's more hurt now than before, and he's going to go after you again because of me."

"I'm big enough to take it." His hands tightened to crushing force on the steering wheel, like he wished they had around Cam's wrist. "Don't worry about me. And don't worry about him. He's not worth the time. *He* hurt *you*, Faith. Over and over. You deserve a guy…" He swallowed hard, knowing he was about to throw away one of the best things to ever happen to him. "You deserve a guy who's honest with you. Who gives you all his attention. Not someone who sees you as a distraction."

She gulped down a shuddering breath. "Could we go somewhere? Just for a minute? If I go home crying, my mom will ask a bunch of questions. And my dad might shoot at you."

"I know just the place."

Chapter Twenty-Eight

Faith should've expected that Cameron would cause a scene, and she knew she shouldn't feel guilty, but she did. Kyle was right. Cameron could've replaced her with any girl and been just fine. Still, the look on his face, the betrayal. It was worse than she'd expected. And Holly had looked like someone had sucked all the air out of her lungs. Faith had a feeling Cam wouldn't have his new girlfriend for long after all that.

Maybe she should've left him sooner, before she'd ended up hurting four people instead of two.

When she nudged that thought, tears welled up in her eyes again. She was embarrassed. Stupidly, foolishly embarrassed. What had gone wrong? This was supposed to be the perfect revenge, and instead she felt like a bitch who had played two guys who hated each other into fighting over her. That hadn't been what she wanted at all, but it's what she deserved.

They turned onto a gravel road, and the Charger bumped its way down to a park. It was dark enough out that Faith couldn't see much more than big trees everywhere, and the sign in the headlights said MORTON ATHLETIC COMPLEX.

"Where are we?" she asked.

He let out a soft, sad laugh. "My Little League fields. Whenever I'm strung out, this place makes me feel better for some reason."

Now she could make out the chain-link fences surrounding the park. Here and there, widely spaced streetlights shone down on the infields—at least four of them. "Did you play select ball?"

"Yeah." He cleared his throat. "It's the only thing I've ever been good at."

"That's not true. You're good at plants." She wiped her eyes on her sleeve, hoping he didn't notice, and added softly, "And winning girls' hearts."

Kyle let out a soft sigh. If she hadn't been straining to hear, she would've missed it. "I'm only good at one of those things, Faith. I'm better at breaking hearts than winning them."

"You haven't broken mine," she said, reaching for his hand.

He let her hold it, but he didn't move to squeeze hers in return. "Yet."

She shook her head, refusing to let go of his hand. "The Kyle I know doesn't seem like a heartbreaker, no matter what you, and the whole school, keep telling me.

His hand finally tightened a little on hers. "I'm nothing like you think. I liked playing a part this week, but tonight made me realize that this isn't going to work. Once we're back in school, I'll go back to being…me, and you're you, so…"

"What are you saying?" Her voice quavered, and she hated it. "Have you been playing me this whole time?"

"No." His tone was firm. "But Faith, you deserve better than me. After tonight, it's probably best that we act like we broke up. Blame me, tell everyone whatever you want. I can take the heat. It'll get Cameron off your back, and things will be better for you."

She let go and sat back in her seat, feeling like she'd taken a bad fall and knocked the air out of her lungs. "You keep saying I deserve better. But so far, all I see is a really nice guy pretending to be an asshole. Why push me away? So far, we seem to be working out pretty well."

He flinched. "Nothing is that simple. Look, I'll only end up hurting you in the long run. If we end it now, it'll be easier."

He sounded hurt. Nothing made sense. Nothing. He'd made her believe it all week long, and now he was pushing her away. "I don't see how."

He wouldn't look at her. "I should probably take you home."

His shoulders were up around his ears, and there were tight lines around his eyes. From the way he crushed the steering wheel in his hands, if she didn't know better, all these signs said he was upset with his decision.

So why do it? Why put a stop to the beginning of a really sweet relationship? Had she done something so wrong to make him give her the old "it's not you, it's me"?

He parked at her curb. Like usual, Dad was sitting in the window, reading. She turned to Kyle. "I don't why you're doing this, and I don't believe the rumors about you are true. I think we could be good together. If you change your mind, I'll listen. But I won't wait around forever."

She got out of the car and slammed her door shut. Despite everything, Kyle waited at the curb until she made it inside. Then he was gone in a sweep of headlights.

Dad stood when she came in. "How was your—pumpkin, are you all right?"

She shook her head. "No. I'd like to go to bed, please."

"Did he hurt you?" Dad growled.

"Not in any way you'd want revenge for." She climbed the

first three stairs slowly. "He doesn't want to see me anymore, that's all. I don't have any idea why."

Dad nodded. "Sometimes teenage boys are idiots."

Tears welled in Faith's eyes, but she laughed. "You're telling me."

"Get some sleep. It'll look better in the morning," he said, reaching up to catch her hand. "It always does."

She nodded and climbed the stairs the rest of the way to her room. Her phone had been vibrating nonstop since they left Dolly's, but she didn't have the heart to wade through all the texts and Snapchat notifications. She set the phone to "do not disturb" and crawled into bed even though it was only eight thirty. She doubted Dad's advice was right, but sleeping off the pain couldn't hurt.

Chapter Twenty-Nine

Kyle took every turn on the winding road to his house too fast, screeching his tires and barely keeping control of his car. He didn't care. He was too hurt, too stupid, too mean to worry about something as simple as keeping the Charger on pavement.

He pushed the speedometer up to eighty. If his dad caught him, he'd be grounded a month. That didn't sound so bad. He'd take a month of house arrest as punishment for what he did to Faith. He hated himself, every last cell, but he had to do it. He *had* to. He couldn't hurt her more by letting her believe in him. She'd hate him more if he tried to keep her, rather than doing the right thing and letting her go before she was too caught up.

He swerved into the driveway and screeched to a halt in front of the garage. The light over the stairs at the front door turned on. Cursing under his breath, he pulled into the garage and climbed out of the car. Once there, though, his feet wouldn't carry him, and he turned to punch the kickboxing bag Dad had given him to work out with. He punched it again. And again, and again.

The automatic lights in the garage shut off, leaving him raging in the dark. He threw himself against the Charger, slamming his back onto the driver's side door, and covered his face with his hands. He ruined everything. Everything. Was his disguise worth it? After Dolly's, Cameron and his buddies were going to be on his ass anyway, and they weren't in eighth grade anymore. Kyle was bigger. Stronger. And now he had his team to back him up. At this point, though, it was three months to graduation. Dropping the act now would screw him over worse. People would look back over the last four years and school would be unbearable. He'd never be able to show his face around town.

Better to forget Faith and finish what he'd started.

The overhead light snapped on. Kyle dropped his hands, worried it was Dad, but Grandpa stood framed in the side door that led to the house. "Kid? What is it?"

Kyle slid down the side of the car and sat on the garage floor. "I blew it, Grandpa."

Grandpa frowned, hitched up his jeans, and walked over to him. It took a little grunting and groaning, but he took a seat on the floor by Kyle. "Tell me about it."

The old man was the only person who understood, so he poured out the whole thing, not sparing himself anything. "So I broke it off with her," he finished, "because I was too goddamned afraid to let go of the fake me. What's wrong with me? Why can't I do it?"

Grandpa patted his shoulder with a heavy hand. "Listen here. Being concerned about what people think of you isn't always a weakness, boy. You've always been a sensitive person, but that's a strength. Most teen guys would do just about anything to nail a girl—including taking advantage and letting her believe in a lie. You aren't like that."

"And I say it *is* a weakness," Kyle snapped. "Being a gentleman is different than being a coward."

"It's gonna happen. At some point, you'll unknot everything that ails you. When the right girl comes along, she'll understand why you did what you did. Okay? Maybe it wasn't to be with the ballerina. Maybe she wasn't the one."

"That's the thing," he muttered. "I think she might've been, but I was too scared she'd hate me for lying to her. That she wanted me because she thought I was something I'm not. If I told her the truth, she was going to turn me loose…and she would've been hurt more because of it."

"Then maybe you should apologize, see where that gets you? Tell her you lost your head a little bit after the show at the ice cream place?" Grandpa scratched the side of his head. "But what do I know? I'm a seventy-one-year-old widower with three lady friends. Maybe I'm not the best person to ask for advice."

Kyle slumped against the car. "I don't mean to be a jackass, Grandpa. You've helped me out so much." He managed a small smile. "I almost broke Cameron Zimmerman's wrist today. He's Faith's ex, cheated on her. He wasn't happy to see her with me."

Grandpa chuckled and smacked his knee. "Bet that little punk thought you'd just roll over and die, did he? We've come a long way since eighth grade, haven't we?"

"Yeah."

Just not far enough.

"Come on inside." Grandpa pushed himself off the floor. "This calls for a beer."

"Uh, you do remember I'm only eighteen, right?"

"Oh, for heaven's sake, of course. But you're a man, whether you feel it or not. And a man drinks a beer when his heart hurts."

Kyle chuckled sadly. "Then your heart must heart a lot, old man."

"Heh, that's only *one* reason why a man drinks a beer. Beer's also good because there's a game on, it's a hot day… and just because."

"Works for me."

Before they went inside, Grandpa squeezed his arm. "You're a good kid, and you're going to be a good man, Kyle. I want you to know I'm proud of you. Every damn day."

Kyle ducked his head so Grandpa wouldn't see the shine of tears in his eyes. "Thanks."

They stood awkwardly for a second before Grandpa snorted. "Okay, enough feelings crap. Let's drink. If you promise not to tell your dad, I'll let you have two beers."

The hard tangle of pain twisted up in his chest loosened a bit. "My lips are sealed."

Thursday morning, Kyle woke up early, forgetting he was almost done with the Gladwells' yard. Good thing he didn't have to be over there right away, because his head was *killing* him. After the first beer, Grandpa decided he needed a boilermaker—and that Kyle did, too. He had to admit, the whiskey shot had made his troubles fade, but now he was regretting ever listening to the old man.

"Never trust a marine, retired or not," he groaned, falling back on his bed. He hadn't been this hungover since that summer he and Cade had sneaked vodka out of Cade's dad's liquor cabinet. They'd thrown up for three hours later that night, trying to hide their dumbassery from his parents by barfing in the neighbor's bushes.

Thinking about Cade made him feel guilty. They used to be best friends, but Kyle hardly talked to him unless Cade came to him first. Baseball took up a lot of his time, sure, but he could've *made* more time. Why had he let eighth grade change him so much? If he hadn't, would he be here now—breaker of Faith's heart because he had problems? A loner with a crowd of friends? A supposed player without a single notch in his belt?

On the other hand, if he hadn't changed, would he have met Faith at all?

That line of questioning felt like it would burn his brain out of his skull…or maybe that was the whiskey chaser. Either way, he had to face the day: he still had practice and work to finish, and the Gladwells hadn't paid him yet. Honestly, if he could avoid going over there, he'd waive the bill, but that would never fly, would it?

He sat up slowly to find four Advil and a big glass of water on his nightstand. A note in Grandpa's handwriting next to it said, *Sorry about that. No…not really.*

Kyle snorted and downed the Advil with a big slug of water. By the time he showered and threw on some athletic shorts and a T-shirt, he could keep his eyes open without squinting. He took the stairs slower than usual, just in case, and went to the kitchen for some toast.

Grandpa was doing a crossword, a big mug of coffee on the table in front of him. "How's the head?"

"As bad as yours, I'd expect." Kyle poured himself some coffee and threw an English muffin into the toaster. "I have to go back over to Faith's. I need to finish their yard."

"You going to talk to her?"

"No." When Grandpa eyed him over the rims of his glasses, Kyle held up his hands. "She's probably pretty pissed at me. I should leave her alone."

"That's an excuse."

"Whatever."

"Hmpf, so you say."

"Yeah, so I say." He leaned against the counter. "I think I might go to Cade's after, if he's home, before practice."

Grandpa brightened at this. "Really? I like that kid. Haven't seen him for a while. Tell him hi for me."

"Will do."

After his breakfast, there was no point in stalling. He coaxed the Toyota out of the garage and drove to the Gladwells' house. Faith's car wasn't in the driveway, and Kyle felt like a coward for being relieved that she wasn't home. Mrs. Gladwell's car was there, though, so he trudged up to the front door and rang the bell.

She came to the door. Nothing about her expression accused of him of hurting her baby. "Kyle! Here to finish up?"

"Yes, ma'am. I just need in the garage to test the sprinklers, then I'll be out of your hair."

Her smile turned sad. "That's too bad. I kind of enjoyed having you around."

She knew, then, and her disappointed expression made him feel about two inches tall. "It's been a good job for me, too."

"Is that all?" she asked, the look in her eye knowing enough that he squirmed.

"Yes," he muttered, looking down at his shoes. "I guess that's all."

"Oh, Kyle." She sighed. "There's a lot I'd like to say, but I promised I wouldn't butt in. Thanks again for all your hard work. While you're fixing the sprinkler, I'll write you a check."

His neck grew hot. He hurt her daughter's feelings, and she was still nice to him—and willing to pay him. This sucked. "Thank you."

When she opened the garage door, he scurried inside gratefully. Guilt clawed its way up his throat, threatening to gag him. He wished he could explain everything to Faith, but with Cameron on the warpath, the best thing he could do for both of them was stay away. She wouldn't suffer for being with him, and he wouldn't have to risk losing everything he'd worked so hard to build.

Part of him wondered, though, if being with Faith was worth the risk. That was selfish thinking, though. There were times he thought she saw right through him, but that didn't matter. He was bad for her. Too messed up in the head and the heart. She deserved more than he could give her.

Still—maybe Grandpa was right. Maybe he should apologize.

He finished up with the sprinkler and knocked on the front door. Mrs. Gladwell appeared, holding a box and an envelope. "The check," she announced, holding up the envelope, "and a special thank-you for all the hard work. The yard is perfect for the luncheon."

"The grass might not be totally rooted by then, so you'll want to be careful where you set up tables." He swallowed hard. "Is, uh, is Faith around?"

"Her play director called everyone to an impromptu brunch with the principal players to lay out the details about rehearsals next week. It's time to start the full cast run-throughs, so he wanted to meet with the stage crew and the principals."

"Ah. Okay, um…" Now what? "Could you tell her…could you tell her I'm sorry?"

Her smile was kind. "I will. Anything else?"

He shook his head, defeat making his bones ache. "No. That's all."

She handed him the box and the check. "It's been nice working with you, hon. I hope to see you again sometime."

He doubted it, but he gave her a polite smile. "Thanks. I better run."

As soon as she closed the door, he jogged to the Toyota, wanting to put distance between himself and this house. In fact, he wanted to put distance between himself and everything his life had become. Frustrated, he drove down to the park where the Little League fields were. There was a trail that wound through the trees around it. He tied his shoes, twisted his torso to stretch his back, and started the timer on his watch.

Without bothering to think about pacing, or distance, or anything really, Kyle took off like he was being chased. Sweat soon stuck his shirt to his back and chest, and his lungs burned, but he didn't stop. He wanted to run until he forgot. Until he was too tired to think. Practice would be extra hard ahead of Tuesday's game, but until then, he needed a release. A runner's high was the only way he thought he could get it.

Grandpa would say he just needed to get laid.

Kyle ran harder, until his breath came in wheezes, before flying into the outfield on one of the Little League fields. He collapsed on the grass and flopped onto his back with his arms over his head. The sky was that pale blue you only saw in spring, and a flock of grackles flew overhead, cawing like the world owed them something. He'd always been so happy here, playing baseball, not worrying about girls, or bullies, or how to hide inside himself for protection. The smell of the grass in the outfield calmed his soul more than anything else.

It wasn't enough, though. He was sick of the lies, the charade. At some point, he needed to reclaim the happy kid he'd been and ditch the surly, confused guy he was. But how? He couldn't just…change and expect no one to question it.

He found himself reaching for his phone. Before he realized it, he was texting Cade. Which could end up being futile, as Cade was the lone guy at Suttonville who still *called* people instead of texting.

K: *You there?*

It took five minutes before the little dots indicating a return message popped up. He imagined Cade staring at the phone, wondering if he should text back or call.

C: *Kyle?*

K: *No, it's your Aunt Tilly.*

C: *Now I know it's you. What's up, man?*

K: *You busy? I need to talk.*

C: *I'm busy with the musical all weekend, but how about Monday after rehearsal? We get out at seven. You can swing by my house.*

The show. That's right—Cade ran AV for the drama classes. That meant he was with Faith. That hurt, but at least he could ask how she was without being obvious.

K: *Yeah, that'll work. See you then.*

His phone rang ten seconds later. "You know what, if you're texting me, I probably ought to make sure you're not standing on a bridge looking down or something."

Kyle laughed at Cade's wry, but suspicious, tone. "I'm lying on my back in the outfield of a Little League field."

"Oh, that's fine, then." Cade paused. "You okay?"

Kyle had to take a long breath before answering to make sure his voice didn't crack. "Not exactly. Girl trouble, you know?"

"You? Girl trouble?" A snort. "Since when?"

"I'm serious, man. There's this girl I really like, but I keep screwing things up. I want to do better for her." God, he sounded stupid. "I need advice."

"What girl?"

"Faith—"

"Gladwell. So the rumors are true." Cade's tone hardened. "You better not screw her over. She's a sweetheart."

"Exactly." Kyle sat up. "That's why I need your help."

"Okay, this is going to take longer than I have right now. Do you mean it?" Cade sounded doubtful. "That you want to do better?"

"Yes. I mean it."

"You know what, I believe you," Cade said. "Step one, be there for her. We'll work out the rest when we talk on Monday."

Kyle's stomach twisted. "That might be easier said than done."

"No excuses. I'll find a way to help you, but you need to own this, or we're done. Got it?"

Funny enough, he did. "Yeah. And thanks."

"You bet. I'll see you Monday. Be good until then."

"I'll try."

Cade hung up, and Kyle stretched back out in the grass. Who knew. Maybe taking a step back to who he was could help him take a giant leap toward who he really wanted to be. Nothing else had worked so far. It was time to see if Cade could work a miracle.

Chapter Thirty

"It's time to work our behinds off, people," Mr. Fisk said. "This could be the best production we've had."

Faith was sure that if the lifts worked, everything else would. She glanced at Josh, the boy playing Jud. He was a pretty good dancer, but she was so worried about him trying to pick her up. He was her height, and thin. Maybe he was stronger than he looked.

"Mr. Fisk?" Cade, the AV boy, asked. "Did you see my email about sepia lighting for the dream sequence?"

"I did. Loved it!" Their teacher looked around at the other principals: Ado Annie, Curly, Jud, Will, and Aunt Eller. "I think we'll be ready to go in two weeks. Your parents will be thrilled."

He had a point—it was a good group. Still, a nagging pain kept tugging at her heart. She'd slept badly last night, but even with Dad saying everything would be better in the morning, it wasn't. Nothing about what happened with Kyle made sense.

It was like…

Like he felt *guilty* for making out with her. But why? *She'd* kissed *him*. It wasn't like he coerced her into it. The whole thing had been so weird. And a little humiliating. Had she been wrong about thinking he was into her?

That couldn't be right, though. Not with the way he looked at her.

This was going to drive her crazy.

"Faith? You with us?"

She looked up, and everyone was staring at her. Mr. Fisk shook his head. "Faith, I asked if you're comfortable with the choreography."

She blinked to refocus on the people around her. "Oh, yeah. Fine. So long as Josh is."

"I'll be fine," he said, giving her a suspicious look.

"All right, then. Cade, I'll see you and the lighting crew at the performing arts hall in an hour. The rest of y'all rest up this weekend—and no stupid activities. If any of you goes mountain biking and shows up with a broken arm next week, I'm going to lose my sh…sanity."

They all laughed and stood to go. Faith bent to check her phone, and when she looked up, she noticed Cade had hung back.

"Need something?" she asked, smiling. He was a nice guy, but they weren't close.

"Can I ask you a question?" He took the seat next to her. "It's kind of personal."

Oh, no. He wasn't going to ask her out, was he? She wasn't ready for that. "Um, sure."

"What's with you and Kyle Sawyer?"

Not him, too. "Why would you ask?"

He frowned. "I thought I heard something, about Dolly's—"

"We were together, but not anymore." She sighed. "He

said he didn't want to anymore. I don't know why."

"Huh." Cade's frown deepened. "Forget I asked. It was kind of rude of me to pry. Guess I'll see you Monday."

He stood and mimed tipping a hat before loping out of the restaurant. He was tall and stocky—the kind of guy who gave great hugs and laughed a lot. Just talking about Kyle made her head hurt, but the look on Cade's face set off an alarm in her head. *Something* happened to drive Kyle away. She just didn't know what, and she was too tired to keep trying to figure it out.

She drove home in her Bug with the top down and the wind in her hair. She really should go to the studio and practice, but the thought of dancing brought back too many feelings. Waiting a few more days would be better. Instead, she drove to Violet's, taking time to enjoy the canopy of trees on the road leading to her house.

Vi flung the front door open before Faith had the Bug in park. "Okay, so what's up with Sawyer?"

That seemed to be the question of the day. "If I knew, I could probably broker world peace." Faith gave Vi a quick hug and followed her inside. The downstairs of her house was wide open, with big picture windows overlooking the lake. She needed this, a moment to recharge. Too many intense things had happened in the last week—not even a week, actually—and it was time to take a step back.

"Well, I, for one, don't believe it." Vi announced. She hopped up onto her coffee table and put her hands on Faith's shoulders. "Look into my eyes, gazelle. That boy is into you. Like a lot. More than Cameron ever was."

Faith tore her gaze away from Violet's. "Even if that was true, he doesn't want me in his life anymore."

Violet let out a theatrical sigh, stepped off the coffee table and flopped onto the couch with a hand flung against her forehead. "Woe is me. I got to make out with an incredibly hot boy, embarrass the hell out of my ex, and now I'm going to let that hot boy scamper out of my life without demanding an explanation." She sat up and pointed at Faith. "Grow a pair, dahling."

Faith threw up her hands. "It's not my decision, and he made it pretty clear he doesn't want me around."

"*Make* it your decision."

Faith sat on the couch next to Violet, who curled up next to her and rested her head on Faith's shoulder. "I have a feeling it's more complicated than that."

"Don't be defeatist. It's ill bred."

Faith groaned. "I'm regretting talking you into bingeing *Downton Abbey* with me."

"It's because I love you." Vi sat up. "Do you want me to find out what's going on? I probably could."

There was no doubt. She had connections in every corner of the school. "I'll think about it over the weekend. I might decide to let it go, but I'll give it serious thought. Promise."

Violet patted her on the head. "Good ballerina. That's a good girl."

Faith laughed. "You keep doing that, and I'm going to wag my tail and demand a treat."

She hopped off the couch. "Treats! I have some. Mom bought six half gallons of ice cream now that Blue Bell is back on sale. She went to three different stores to find them. I say we eat it all up."

Faith followed her into the kitchen. "Now you're talking."

"Faith?" Mom called when she opened the front door.

It sounded like she was on the porch. Faith's heart panged. Beautiful as the yard was, she wasn't sure she wanted to see it—or Kyle—right now. She'd eaten two bowls of ice cream and wanted nothing more than to take a bath and lie in bed reading for three hours.

"Faith? I want to talk to you."

Persistent mothers were akin to attention-seeking three-year-olds: they wouldn't stop chasing you down until they got their way. "Coming."

The porch was bathed in light from the setting sun, and the azaleas glowed. No sign of Kyle, though. She'd guessed that, since his truck wasn't here, but there was always a chance. Mom motioned for her to come sit on the sofa with her.

"So I take it things didn't work out with Kyle?" she asked.

Dad must've talked to her. "No. He decided he wasn't interested."

Mom stroked her hair. "Hmm. Why would that be?"

Faith fought the urge to bury her face in Mom's lap and cry until her tears were dried up. There were advantages to being a four-year-old, back when things were uncomplicated and a skinned knee was the worst thing that could happen. "He said he'd break my heart if we stayed together. I should've seen that coming, actually. Breaking hearts is his specialty."

Mom's forehead wrinkled. "Kyle? Our Kyle?"

Our Kyle, like she'd already adopted him and made a place for him at their dinner table. "Yes."

"But why would you think that?"

"Mom, I didn't want to tell you this because I thought you'd worry, and I can take care of myself. Kyle's a total player. He's kind of a bad boy, actually. Races his Charger, gets into trouble a lot, has a string of college-aged girls on the go."

Mom's expressed went from confused to flabbergasted. "Honey, there's no way that kid is all those things. He's so professional." She chuckled. "When he's not being socially awkward, that is. That is *not* a boy who dumps girls after one date or runs with a bad crowd. Didn't you say he plays baseball?"

"Yeah, and he's really good." Faith picked at her fingernails. "He's an outfielder. Apparently he takes crazy dives all the time. So even on the field, he's wild."

"'Wild' isn't the word I'd use," Mom said, taking her hand so she had to stop tearing up her nails. "'Fierce,' maybe? 'Passionate'? One look at our backyard will tell you that—what Kyle loves, he does with everything he has. Which is why I'm so surprised he broke it off with you."

"Mom, we hung out together for five days. Love has nothing to do with it."

"Maybe not now, but he seems like the type of guy who knows what he likes, and latches onto it, all in." She kissed the side of Faith's forehead. "I'm as in the dark as you are. And I'm sorry it turned out this way. I liked him. Your dad did, too. That's saying something."

Faith couldn't remember dating anyone her father approved of, which made all this even worse. She wouldn't have worried about Kyle's reputation one bit if he'd kept treating her like she mattered. Like she was *special*. That's what made this so frustrating—even after five days, she could see a future with him. Maybe not forever, but definitely past graduation. She'd been so infatuated with this guy, to the point that she thought he could've been the one—the guy she could finally say she cared about enough to take that next step. That if he had asked, she would've slept with him.

And wouldn't have regretted a thing.

Blood rushed to her cheeks, and her heart ached. She would've given him anything, everything he wanted. A rational person would be ashamed of that, probably, but she was nothing but hurt. This stung more than seeing Cameron in bed with Holly.

She stood and turned her back on the yard. "I guess he fooled all of us."

Chapter Thirty-One

When school started Monday morning, people stared at Faith everywhere she went. Lots of whispering, lots of laughter behind her back.

She didn't care. None of it mattered anymore.

Violet stopped her at her locker. "You okay?"

"Fine." Faith slammed her locker door shut. "Peachy."

"Girl…"

"I'll be okay," she said. "Although I heard Cameron is looking to beat Kyle up after school."

"Good luck with that," Vi said. "He'll be at baseball practice. Only an idiot would pick a fight with a guy who has access to friends with bats."

"We're talking about Cam."

"Oh, right. Then I hope he succeeds in finding Kyle. A beating would do him good."

"Just so long as he lands a punch or two."

Vi put a hand on her hip. "What happened?"

Faith shook her head. When she walked into school that morning, she'd passed right by Kyle. He'd smiled briefly at her, like a casual friend would, but didn't say anything. That hurt, but if she told Violet, her best friend would take on Cameron's quest—an enemy of my enemy is my friend, so to speak. "It's nothing. Just all the gossip."

"Ignore it. The scheme did what it was supposed to do. You aren't getting nasty texts from football players anymore, are you?"

"Only a few." Faith snorted. "I got twelve more asking if I'd meet up with them for lunch or coffee. Apparently, I'm now the school slut, which is laughable."

"It's going to be fine." Vi gave her arm a bracing pat. "See you at lunch?"

"Sure."

The day didn't get any better, though. She was so preoccupied, she failed a pop quiz in political science, and couldn't find her homework in English. When she walked into Spanish, Holly Masterson hissed, "Bitch," as she passed by.

Faith waved a hand, exhausted with the fight. "Whatever."

Snickers ran around the room and Señora Cabraya gave everyone a stern look. "Seats, *por favor.*"

Faith went to her desk, wondering if there'd ever be an end to this godforsaken day.

When school finally let out, she only had an hour to run home, do homework, and be back up to the performing arts center for rehearsal, but there was no way she was staying at school. She dashed out to her car before most people had cleared their lockers. She hadn't seen Kyle since that morning, which wasn't a surprise—the school was huge. Still, she half wondered if he was avoiding her.

She let herself in through the garage door. A pile of mail sat on the kitchen table, as usual, but there was a letter sitting at her place. A letter with NYU's logo on it.

She approached the letter with caution, heart hammering. The envelope was thin. What did that mean? Was it good news? Or bad? She reached for it with shaking hands and tore open the end.

Dear Ms. Gladwell,

Thank you for your interest in the New York University musical theater program. Your audition was reviewed by a panel of three tenured faculty. Unfortunately, we are unable to extend you an admission at this time. You may audition again next year. We wish you all the best in your future endeavors.

Sincerely,
Dr. J. Rabin

The letter dropped to the floor, falling from numb fingers. They passed on her. She wasn't going to NYU. They didn't want her. She wasn't good enough.

Tears welled up in her eyes, and every nerve was raw with pain. What was she going to do? Where would she go now? None of the Texas schools that accepted her had musical theater programs that compared with NYU.

With a cry, she snatched the letter off the floor and crumpled it into a tiny ball. She still had to go to rehearsal and perform tonight like nothing mattered. The show must go on, or some shit like that. But all she wanted to do was crawl into bed and cry while letting her dream go. Mom wasn't even home to give her a comforting hug.

Faith went out to the porch and wiped her eyes. The backyard and all its colors mocked her grief. She wished she could pull up every azalea. Tear them apart with her bare hands...

Her shoulders slumped. No, she didn't want that. No matter how Kyle ignored her, no matter how awful this day was, the yard was beautiful, and she couldn't ruin it, even though everything else was.

She shoved the letter deep into the kitchen trash can so her parents wouldn't find it before she could tell them herself, which she didn't feel like doing, yet. There had to be some time to absorb it first, so she could talk about this without sobbing. She did her homework methodically, not really seeing, or caring, the answers she put down. When she realized she'd been reading the same page of *Julius Caesar* over and over, she finally gave it up. She'd seen the play twice, and that would have to do. Better to go on to practice early than waste her time.

She shoved every angry, upset, painful feeling down deep and drove back to school. In the distance, she could see small figures running laps around the baseball field. Kyle was out there somewhere, but he didn't care about her, or her drama, anymore. She wasn't worth his time. Or NYU's. No matter how many times people told her she was special, turned out she wasn't special *enough*.

She clutched her dance bag close, hunching over it, and walked briskly into the rehearsal hall.

Cade smiled and waved from the soundboard at the back of the theater. She was too upset to smile, but she nodded. His smile faded and he rose. "You okay?"

"Fine," she said. "Just got some bad news is all."

"Are you sure that's all?"

His face was so kind. Cade was one of those boys who was funny and sweet and totally underrated. He also had a way of making you trust him on sight. Why couldn't she fall for a guy like him?

Maybe that's why she said, "I didn't get accepted to NYU. Please don't tell the others."

He nodded. "I won't. I know how they can be. And Faith? I'm so sorry."

She blinked back tears. "Me, too."

She made her way down to the stage where Mr. Fisk was practicing a solo with Jenny, the girl who play Ado Annie. Faith couldn't help but smile. Jenny sounded exactly like Gloria Grahame, the woman who'd played her in the classic 1955 version, nasal twang, fake innocent expression and all. Funny how Faith had pretended to be a girl who "cain't say no" to the bad boy of Suttonville, and still didn't end up with a happy ending like Ado Annie.

They finished and Mr. Fisk spotted her. "Faith, come warm up, honey. How about 'People Will Say We're in Love?'"

Her stomach clenched. "Not sure I'm in the mood for that one, Mr. Fisk."

He gave her a sympathetic look. Her drama teacher was well connected with gossip, so he probably knew some, if not all, of what happened the last week. "Then 'Many a New Day.'" He smiled. "Everyone deserves a do-over."

She smiled, knowing full well it was weak. "That's fine."

"Cade, could you reset the board for Faith please? Drop channel seven. We won't need it."

"Will do!" Cade's disembodied voice called from the sound booth at the back of the theater.

Mr. Fisk waved her over to the piano. "Jenny's great, but she doesn't have the power you do."

Power, as if. She had no power at all. Still, she wasn't going to blow a performance for any finicky guy or mean university. She did a few quick vocal warm-ups, then nodded to her teacher. He started the intro on the piano.

The song was about a girl who had been courted and flirted with by a man who teased her. The girl, to teach him a lesson, agreed to go to a shindig with his rival. In retaliation, the man she really loved invited another girl to go with him. Now she was singing about how she didn't care, that she would move on. But in the end, Laurey *couldn't* move on. And she ended up hurt. The song was as much about new beginnings as it was about painful endings.

When she finished singing, she focused back on everything around her. Her cheeks were wet, and half the cast, along with most of the orchestra, had arrived. All of them were watching, and when the last piano note died, everyone started clapping.

Mr. Fisk gave her arm a squeeze and motioned her close. "You're as strong as Laurey, honey. Don't you forget that."

She nodded and went to take her place with the cast, hurriedly drying her tears on her sleeve. Just like the song, she'd start all over again.

They practiced most of the first act without any mishaps, other than Mr. Fisk stopping the orchestra teacher once or twice to adjust the pit's tone or volume. Once when Faith wandered too close to the edge of the stage, a bass player waved his bow at her, grinning from ear to ear. They were having a great time down there. It thawed some of the icy pain around her heart.

Drama kids and musicians were her people.

After a break, Mr. Fisk called, "I want to block Laurey's nightmare ballet with the full cast and chorus to see how spacing looks with the dance elements. That way we can do a full Act I run-through tomorrow. Laurey, Jud, center stage, please."

Faith changed into her pointe shoes, then walked over to Josh as the chorus dancers surrounded them. "Ready?"

He shrugged. "My part's not that hard."

Anger burned like a banked coal in her chest. "Good. Then don't screw it up."

"Places!" Mr. Fisk called from the fifth row. "Orchestra, start from the beginning. Faith, remember you're bewildered and increasingly horrified."

That shouldn't be a problem. She took her place stage left, and Josh crossed to stage right and hooked his thumbs into his waistband. His smug expression faded into a hard, dominating expression. Almost too believable.

Faith raised her arms into fourth position and tilted her head. Bewildered. Afraid. Grieving. Oh, she had that down. She widened her eyes and parted her lips as two saloon girls did a mocking cancan on either side of Josh, who had now become Jud in her eyes.

The dancers moved aggressively her direction. *Relevé, pirouette away*. Elevé, *skitter to the back of the stage. Be afraid, Laurey. Be very afraid. He's going to hurt you.*

Her heart pounded—the fear felt too real. Three cowboys jigged around her, and she clapped her hands to her head and spun in the opposite direction. Jud knocked them away and reached for her. She leaped, landed, took three flutter steps, then jumped into a full split, crossing the stage mostly in the air. Jud stalked after her again, and the mocking cancan girls walked behind him, sneering and smirking.

She backed up, spinning, and bumped into the cowboys, who took three menacing steps forward, forcing her toward Jud. Goose bumps rose on her arms, and real horror crept up her throat. She couldn't disassociate herself from Laurey anymore.

Josh grabbed her around her waist and pulled her roughly against him. Faith went up on her toes and arched her back as he spun them in a circles. At the end of the third spin, he gave her a little shove, sending her twirling into the cowboys. They laughed and spun her right back. Faith bunched her muscles, took a step, and leaped into Josh's arms.

He was supposed to catch her waist and lift her above his head—the easiest of their three lifts this scene. Just a quick up, then down. Instead he staggered back and dropped her.

Faith barely kept her balance and landed hard on her heels. Mr. Fisk yelled, "Cut!"

"What was that?" she asked.

Josh shrugged. "Sorry. You're heavy."

The two cancan girls rolled their eyes and one said, "She's got muscle tone, but she's not even close to heavy, you jackass."

"Shut up, Alyssa." He turned to glare at Faith. "Whose idea was it to put lifts in this thing, anyway?"

"Mine," Mr. Fisk snapped. "And you told me you could do it. Can you?"

"I'm not sure."

Mr. Fisk muttered under his breath before pointing at Josh. "Run it again. Anticipate the move. Faith's giving you momentum with her jump. You just have to carry her the rest of the way up." He sighed. "All the same, we probably should remove the fish lift. I'll work out something else."

Faith's face burned. Heavy? Sure, she had muscle tone, like Alyssa said, but she'd never thought of herself as heavy. Was that what NYU saw when they watched her audition? A ballerina with a pretty voice, who couldn't be lifted by a typical musical theater student? A girl who could jump, but couldn't fly?

They went through the scene again and again. Josh managed to lift her twice, but he dropped her one other time, and fell over, carrying her with him on the last try.

"Cut," Mr. Fisk called wearily. "That's it for tonight. Go home, rest up. Josh, Faith, make sure you stretch and find some Icy Hot for those bruises."

Everyone scattered. Rehearsal had been a disaster, and no one wanted to stick around. Faith lingered on the stage, trying to stop feeling defeated. "Mr. Fisk? Can I stay? I want to work out a few things to modify the scene for tomorrow."

Lights were already being turned off around the theater. Mr. Fisk glanced back at Cade. "I wish I could say yes, but I'm late for something. Can it wait until tomorrow?"

Tears welled in her eyes, so she stared at her pointe shoes. "Okay."

"Mr. Fisk? I can stay," Cade called from his dark audio nook. "I have a key. If you're okay with that, Faith?"

Mr. Fisk looked torn, but Faith jumped on it. "That would be great."

"All right," he said. "I'm trusting you two. Only one hour, got it? Then lock up and head home before your parents write me nasty emails for cutting into homework time."

She nodded. "Thanks."

He walked out and Cade said, "You ready?"

She took her place center stage and he turned off most of the lights except for a spotlight right on her. The seats disappeared and she was alone in a sea of darkness.

"What song? I have all the recordings back here," Cade called. "The nightmare sequence?"

She swallowed down the last of her tears. "'People Will Say We're in Love.'"

Chapter Thirty-Two

KYLE

Kyle headed to practice early, leaving most of the team joking around in the locker room. Seeing Faith in the hall this morning had rattled him more than he expected it to. He'd spent the rest of the day with his hood pulled up whenever he could get away with it, and his earbuds in. It didn't stop him from hearing the rumors flying all around him, though, until he almost couldn't take it anymore.

All he could think was, *what have I done?* He needed the green of the field to clear his head and set him straight.

On his way out of the locker room, a few guys were waiting outside the chain link fence surrounding the field. Cameron, flanked by two of his football buddies. The three of them were glaring right at Kyle, so they must be there for him. What a surprise.

Actually, it kind of *was*—the rest of the baseball team would be out any second. What did they think they could do to him on his turf? He decided to play it cool. "What's up?"

Cameron leaned against the fence. "You need to stay away from Faith."

Showed what he knew, but he wasn't going to give Cameron a reason to think *he* pushed Faith away from him. "Yeah? And why's that? Last I heard, she wasn't taken."

Out of nowhere, two more guys grabbed his arms from behind and slammed him into the fence. Cameron got in his face, glaring at him. "Because you're not good enough for her. You know it, I know it. Leave her alone."

Kyle struggled, pushing against the guys holding him, but they didn't let up. The chain links from the fence ground against his face. "You don't have a say. She's her own person, asshole. She has the right to go out with anyone she wants. Or are you just mad she went after me?"

"You're nothing but a loser, Sawyer." Cameron poked him hard in the chest. "Leave her alone, or next time I'll hurt more than your pride."

"What in the Sam Hill is going on out here!" Coach shouted.

Footsteps pounded, and the guys holding him abruptly let go. The three guys on the outside of the fence ran for it, but Tristan had the other two by the backs of their shirts—underclassmen by the looks of it. They glared defiantly at him.

"Simons, Carrier." Coach sounded disgusted. "I don't know what that was about, but I have zero tolerance for fighting. If you paid attention in my history class, you would've remembered that."

"We weren't fighting, sir." Simons jerked free of Tristan's grip. "We were just talking."

"With Sawyer slammed up against the fence?" Coach's eyes lit up with anger. "Get off my field, both of you. I'll see you in the principal's office tomorrow—if you're lucky, you'll only get three days' in-school suspension."

"But—" Carrier said.

"Go. Now." Coach turned his back on them, trusting the rest of the team to take care of the problem.

"You heard him," Tristan said cheerfully. "Off you go!"

The rest of the team herded Carrier and Simons out the gate at the edge of the field, and many of them watched until they disappeared into the parking lot. A moment later, tires squealed.

Tristan turned to Kyle. "What, is Cam a Mafia boss or something? Or is he so afraid of you he had to bring four guys to keep you away from Faith?"

"How do you know that's what he wanted? Maybe he wanted to kick my ass just because." Kyle rubbed at his cheek. He'd have a weird octagonal bruise across his cheekbone tomorrow. That would be a tough one to explain to Grandpa.

Tristan rolled his eyes. "Warning off the guy who made out with his ex in public? I'd say it's *all* about Faith."

Kyle didn't answer.

"All right, guys. Enough chitchat. We have a game tomorrow." Coach checked his stopwatch. "Let's do some sprint drills."

Everybody groaned and lined up. Kyle took a few slow breaths. The adrenaline from the ambush still roared through his veins, so when Coach shouted, "Go!" he took off like a shot. Back and forth from home to first, touching the bases at each end, not counting how many turns, or seconds, or anything. He just ran, trying to focus his roiling mind.

"Stop!" Coach was shaking his head. "Sawyer, you made eighteen turns. Save some of that speed for tomorrow, kid. Starters, head out for catching drill. The rest of you are on the batting machine."

Kyle went to the dugout for his mitt, overhearing one of the better freshman players mutter, "With Sawyer here, I'm never gonna play. He's an iron man."

Kyle felt a little bad for the kid, but not much. He was

graduating—this was his last season. He paused and turned to the wide-eyed freshman. "Ledecky, you'll play next year. And you'll probably be better than me in the long run. Your turn is coming."

Ledecky's astonished smile made him feel a little better, but only for a second. One thing Cam had said kept ringing in his ears: *you're not good enough for her*. He already knew that, but it stung to hear someone else say it. Angry, he ran onto the field, spending the next sixty minutes fielding everything sent his way. By the time Coach waved them over, the front of his practice jersey was almost entirely green with grass stains.

He jogged down the steps to the dugout, where Tristan was waiting for him. He looked ready to bite a nail in half. "Want me to walk you to your car?"

Kyle shook his head. "Nah. I'm going to stay, do a little extra batting practice."

"Don't push it. But, seriously, we got your back, man." Tristan punched his shoulder. "They mess with you, they mess with all of us. You don't have to haul it alone, okay?"

Tristan had played ball with him on one team or another since they were eleven. He remembered what life had been like. And he didn't care. He still had Kyle's back.

Kyle wasn't alone.

He squared his shoulders. "Thanks. And I have your back, too."

A fastball flew out of the pitching machine. Kyle let instinct take over and swung. No contact. Damn, too high. He squared up in the batter's box again. The next pitch came and this time he connected, nice and hard. The ball sailed up, up, up, and sailed over the fence.

"Sawyer," Coach called. "Time to shut down. Almost

everyone else is gone."

Another ball came. Another solid hit to the left field corner. Double.

Coach went to the pitching machine and turned it off. "That's enough. You're looking good—don't overdo it and hurt yourself."

"Okay." He took a long breath and raised his arms over his head to stretch his shoulders. "I'm out, then."

"See you tomorrow. Get some sleep, will you? You look exhausted. I need my players sharp."

Kyle nodded, packed up his gear, and walked out to his car. Someone had thrown an egg at the Charger. Cursing under his breath, he set to wiping it off with one of his towels. Seriously, couldn't Cameron be more creative? At least they hadn't slashed his tires.

His phone buzzed right as he started the car. Cade.

"Yeah?"

"It's me."

"I kind of gathered that from the caller ID. We still on for tonight? I should probably go shower first."

"I need you at the theater. Now."

"Why? Something wrong?"

"I'll explain when you get here. Meet me by the front door. How long?"

Kyle glanced over at the main campus. "I'm just at the ball field. So…two minutes?"

Cade's hand must've covered the phone, because there was a crackle, then it sounded like he was talking to someone. "Okay, I'm back. Two minutes is great. I'll reset this song and be right out."

Kyle hung up, frowning. The theater? This had something to do with Faith, but what? Cade had sounded worried, like something was wrong. He put the Charger in gear and sped to the other side of the school as fast as the speed bumps would let him. When he pulled up, Cade frantically waved him inside.

"I told her I was talking a quick call. We need to hurry." Cade glanced down at his feet. "You're wearing cleats? This is going to be interesting."

"I just came from practice. What's this all about?"

"Remember how I said step one was to be there for Faith? This is your cue—she's rock-bottom devastated, man." Cade ushered him inside, and instead of taking him into the theater, led him down a side hall to a door that said CAST ONLY.

Kyle's pulse picked up ten beats a minute. "Devastated? About what?"

Cade grimaced. "She didn't get into NYU. Josh dropped her like, ten times during rehearsal. She's catching a lot of shit at school after y'all's stunt. Pick one."

Kyle closed his eyes, an ache beginning behind his breastbone. "What am I going to do but make it worse?"

"Make it better." Cade gave him a shove. "For God's sake, just try. She needs a knight in shining armor. Don't disappoint her. Now, I've put the music on a loop of three songs. I'll be in the AV room for the next thirty minutes. That's your window. Now go!"

Cade didn't give him time to protest, spinning on his heel and heading the opposite direction before Kyle could even open his mouth. He leaned against the wall and let his head fall against it. Strains of music from *Oklahoma!* floated through the door, and a clear sweet voice started singing, "Many a New Day."

He leaned over and cracked the door to hear better. Goose bumps rose on his arms when she hit the high notes. God, she was amazing. How could a girl like this *not* be accepted into NYU?

She made it halfway through the song, then stopped. For a moment, he thought it was a pause for the chorus to sing... until he heard her crying.

He pulled open the door. It squeaked, and Faith drew in a sharp breath. "Cade?"

Knight in shining armor. Right. He plodded up the stairs at the side of the stage, wincing at how loud his cleats rang against the metal steps, and pulled back the curtain. "Not exactly."

She wrapped her arms around her middle. "What are you doing here? And where's Cade?"

"Cade and I are friends. He called to say you were having a rough day and asked…" A self-deprecating smile spread across his face. "*Told* me I needed to come over and check on you. He's out doing some work on the AV system."

Faith avoided his gaze, staring at spot on the stage floor. "Oh."

Kyle stepped up onto the stage. The scarred wooden floor creaked under his cleats, and he was painfully aware that he'd shown up here in baseball pants and a tight Under Armour sleeveless shirt, having left his practice jersey in the car. Maybe he should've changed.

Then again, Faith was wearing a leotard covered by a fluffy skirt that went past her knees and ballet shoes. He nodded at the skirt. "You have some interesting workout clothes."

She blushed. "And you're wearing cleats in a theater. I think we're even."

"Yeah." He crossed the stage, stopping a few feet away from her. "So what's going on?"

Faith shook her head. "It's nothing."

"I know that's not true. Cade wouldn't have called if it was nothing." He took a step toward her. "Want to talk about it? We're the only ones here."

Her lower lip trembled, and she clenched her hands together. "I…"

She burst into tears and covered her face. Kyle cleared the distance between them in one big step and wrapped his arms around her. She stood stiff against him, but he rubbed her back in slow circles until she relaxed enough to cry on his shoulder.

"Tell me what to do," he whispered into her hair. "Tell me and I'll do it. Even if you want me to go."

"I don't want you to go." Her voice vibrated against his collarbone, and chills raced down his back.

"I'm not going anywhere, then."

They stood together, center stage, and while Faith finished crying, Kyle breathed in her scent: sweat, citrus, chalk she used to fix the floor when she danced. This girl was inside his head. Could he tell her the truth?

Just the thought made his hands shake. He gave her a final pat and let her go. She sniffed for another few seconds and wiped her eyes. "Thank you. For coming."

"I'd do anything for you," he said, hating the tiny tremor in his voice. Some knight he was, terrified of a damsel in distress. "Anything."

She peered up at him, her expression shy. "Can you dance in the musical?"

He laughed. "I could, but I'm not sure the cast would like that."

"Josh can't lift me. He says I'm too *heavy*." Tears welled up over her eyelashes again. "NYU rejected me. Do you think that's why? That I'm too heavy? Or too tall? Or is it my voice? My dancing?"

"Faith, it's none of those things. I've seen you dance, and now I've heard you sing." He reached for her arms, gripping them tightly. "It's like professional sports—sometimes the break comes because of luck. You are a great singer, a beautiful dancer, and you sure as *hell* aren't too heavy." He shook his head in disgust. "This Josh needs to do some weight training if he can't lift you, especially if you're doing half the work by jumping first."

She nodded, blinking back tears, but looked too choked up to say anything.

Not good enough.

He released her arms and moved five steps back. "Is that lift we tried the other night the hardest one?"

She shook her head. "There's a more difficult one."

"Tell me what to do."

Her eyes flew open wide. "You want to dance with me? Wait. What about the other day? You pushed me away, Kyle. Why are you here?"

The words were on the tip of his tongue: *I'm scared. I want to be with you but I don't know how. I'm not good enough for you. I'm a liar, even to myself.*

He sighed. "You need me."

The answer wasn't adequate, he knew that, and her frustrated expression confirmed his fears. She squared her shoulders, though. "This one requires more work on your part."

Relieved she'd stopped crying, he flexed his biceps. "I think I can handle it."

Her face went scarlet, and she gave him a quick smile. "I'm telling you—we need you on this stage."

He grinned. "Not gonna happen. Now, about this lift."

"It's called a fish lift," she said. "The easier version is to dip me in the hold, which is what Josh is supposed to do. The harder way is to lift me over your head." She glanced at the wooden floor. "We'll stick to the dip."

Showing off and lifting her over his head sounded like a good idea, but giving her a concussion if he dropped her didn't. "Fair enough."

"Okay, so I'm going to turn in to you. When I do, bend your knees a little and get an arm around my waist. When my back leg comes up…" She bit her bottom lip. "Um, grab my thigh. About midway up."

"Your thigh. Fine." This was sounding better and better. "Anything else?"

"Once you have me off the floor, I'll hold my pose. You dip my head and do a turn, then bend your knees and I'll step out of the hold."

He clapped his hands. "Okay, Gladwell. Bring it on."

She rolled her eyes, but her smile was back, and that was all that mattered. "One, two, three."

She spun toward him on her toes, and he grabbed her waist. Her back leg came up, just like she described, and he caught it, trying to ignore the lean strength of the thigh muscle in his hand. Her free leg bent so that her foot touched her opposite knee, and she held her arms out, graceful and sure.

"Dip!" she commanded.

He tilted her head down, turned in a circle, then let her go. "Piece of cake."

She beamed. "Not too many guys can do that lift. That's part of why I'm still here." She grimaced. "I'm working on new choreography to take the lifts out."

She went to the edge of the stage and sat, dangling her legs into the orchestra pit. Kyle joined her. "That's too bad."

"It is, but at least I was able to try it with someone." She reached for his hand. "Thank you."

"What about NYU?" he asked, not daring to move his hand, afraid she'd let go.

She stared out into the dark auditorium. "I'll go in-state somewhere. North Texas has a great vocal department. Maybe I'll try their program instead."

Faith sounded—and looked—so tired. Kyle scooted closer and put an arm around her shoulders. "And maybe in a year, you can try to go to NYU again. Or find an agent and make your own way."

"Maybe." She turned her head, and their faces were only inches apart. "You always know how to make me feel better."

"I try."

"You do, and that's why this doesn't make sense. Why did you push me away? You avoided the question earlier."

Now it was his turn to stare out at the auditorium. He knew his palm was getting sweaty in hers, and an alarm in his head shouted, *Get out! Get out!* "I don't think I'm...good boyfriend material."

"That's a cop-out." She reached out and turned his face back to hers. "And I can prove it."

Before he could say anything—or blink—she pressed her lips against his.

Chapter Thirty-Three

Faith put every bit of frustration, confusion, grief, and longing behind the kiss, and she wasn't surprised at all when Kyle thawed out and kissed her back. This day had epically sucked, and she needed to take it out on someone.

This seemed like a good way to do it.

He pulled away. "We're not exactly in the safest place. We're kind of hanging over a bottomless pit."

"What, you don't like kissing me, hanging over a bottomless pit?" She pushed herself to her feet. "And it's not *that* bottomless. Musicians sit in there and don't complain."

He stood. "They must be braver than I am."

"Maybe." She took his hand and tugged him across the stage and behind the curtain. Sets rested along the walls, and dust, costume scraps, and discarded script pages littered the floor. It was dark and quiet, though. And private. "How about here?"

He looked confused. "What about here?"

"To kiss me."

"Are you sure that's what we should be doing?"

Faith wound her arms around his neck. "Definitely. I'm a girl who needs kissing, and badly."

He untangled her arms and for a second, she thought she felt his hands shake. But then his face did that closed-off thing she hated. "Or maybe you've had a really awful day and you aren't thinking this through."

She put her hands on her hips. "Is it me? Am I not good enough for you?"

"I think we both know that's not true." He looked away. Shifted from foot to foot like he wanted to be anywhere but there.

"No." Her temper flared. Maybe kissing wasn't what she needed after all. Maybe she needed to vent to someone. "This shutting-down crap has to stop. Either you want to be with me, or you don't."

"I'm not doing this with you right now."

He turned to go, and the dam broke on her frustration. "We're all messed up inside, Kyle. All of us have baggage. Why won't you let me in?"

He stopped but didn't turn around. "Because this is who I am."

"And I think that's bullshit." She stared at his back. His fists were clenched...and shaking. She sucked in a breath. "This isn't about us at all, is it? It's about you. Look, there's nothing so bad that I won't understand. Let me try. You can trust me."

He shook his head, and his shoulders slumped. "I can't trust anyone."

Kyle left her. The door squeaked as it opened, and slammed shut a second later.

The only sound left was the swish of the curtain against the floor.

"He did what?" Violet yelled. Her face was purple with fury. She'd come over as soon as Faith broke down trying to tell her what happened.

Faith waved a hand, hoping she looked as unaffected as Kyle. Too bad she *was* affected. "It's over now. He can go be broody and dark somewhere else."

"Says the girl with tearstains on her face and a runny nose." Vi cracked her knuckles. "He better stay clear of me the next few days."

"Why would he think he can't trust anyone?" Faith rubbed at her eyes. "God, things are so messed up right now."

Vi put her arm around Faith's shoulder and snuggled close. "They are, but you're strong and you can take it."

Her heart throbbed painfully. "Are you sure?"

"I am." Violet stood and brushed Faith's hair off her forehead. "You know…"

Faith's eyes narrowed. "What?"

She sighed. "He fooled me, too."

After a quick hug, she trotted downstairs, leaving Faith alone. Anytime Vi left a room, there was a void, like all the good mojo left with her. Faith sank down on her bed, hugging a pillow. She hadn't imagined it, then. Kyle had been attracted to her, and not just as a quick hookup or disposable girl.

For some reason, knowing that made the rejection hurt worse.

Her phone buzzed on her nightstand. She reached for it, thinking Vi had forgotten something, but it buzzed again, and again. Someone was calling instead of texting, but she didn't recognize the number.

She allowed the call. "Hello?"

"Faith?" a slightly out-of-breath male voice asked.

"Yeah." She frowned. "Cade?"

"Oh, good. I was worried you might think I was a creeper and hang up."

She smiled despite her mood. "No one could ever think you're a creeper."

"That depends on whether or not Scarlett Johansson got all ninety-seven of my letters."

Faith's mouth dropped open. "Uh, what?"

"I kid, I kid," he said. "Faith, I called to apologize. I never should've asked Kyle to come tonight."

He sounded so upset, she forgave him immediately. "You thought you were doing something helpful. And that's sweet."

"On my part, maybe." Cade sounded bitter, so unlike him. "I'd hoped…never mind. It doesn't matter so much now."

"What did you hope?" she asked cautiously.

There was a long pause. "I hoped Kyle might pull himself together. He'd lose his ever-loving shit if he knew I was telling you this, but he doesn't know what to do with his feelings, so he stuffs them in a jar."

"Are we talking about Kyle Sawyer?" she asked. "Badass, I-bone-college-girls, loner Kyle?" Even saying it sounded fake.

Cade laughed. "One and the same. Anyway, I wanted you to know how sorry I am."

"Don't be." Cade's saying Kyle stuffed his feelings away matched her own suspicions. What could possibly be so bad that he felt like he had to shut everyone out—shut *her* out?

She sighed. No matter how frustrated he made her, she couldn't stop caring. "Is he okay?"

Cade laughed again. This time there was a wry quality to it, like he was letting her in on a joke. "No, but after I'm through with him, he might be."

He hung up, and Faith dropped her phone on the bed, feeling like pieces of a puzzle were falling into place, but also knowing she might never have the whole picture.

Chapter Thirty-Four

Kyle was nearly home when Cade called. "Where the hell are you?"

He pulled into the long driveway leading up to their house, but stopped. "Home. Why?"

"You were supposed to come over. You're not getting out of this." Cade sounded more steamed than Kyle had ever heard. "My house. Fifteen minutes."

He hung up before Kyle could give him an excuse. Kyle rested his head against the steering wheel. Why couldn't he trust himself enough to open up to Faith? What was *wrong* with him? A corner of his heart beat out her name over and over and over, and he knew what he should do, but he couldn't figure out how. No, that wasn't right—he didn't know how to do it without pain. Without saying, outright, that he'd lied to her.

Sighing, he backed out of the driveway. He'd wanted a miracle, right? Time to suck it up and see what his old friend had in store.

Cade wrenched the door open as soon as Kyle set foot on their porch. He was frowning. "Can you be honest with me? Before we go through this, are you really going to talk to me, or are we gonna dance? Because I gave you some specific instructions and you didn't listen. In fact, you made things worse."

Kyle's bones ached, and he was tired all over. What was it his grandpa always said when he was being a cagey bastard? *The truth will set you free.* Yeah, it was time to lose his burdens. "I'm here to talk."

Cade nodded sharply. "Step into my office."

Cade's mouth was hanging open. They'd stolen a bag of Chips Ahoy, a gallon of milk, and two glasses from his kitchen, and gone straight to the game room. When Cade asked why Kyle had walked out on Faith, something broke inside him. Cade had the kind of face that begged you to tell him your troubles, and the sum of four years of pain had come pouring out. Kyle had thought he'd feel ashamed, telling someone other than Grandpa, but Cade hadn't mocked him, not once.

If anything, he looked like someone had bashed him in the face with a two-by-four.

"Wow, dude. That's…that's…" Cade shook himself. "Okay, you know me, right?"

Kyle snorted. "Yeah, I know you. I wouldn't share this tale with a random stranger, not even if he brought cookies and milk. Thanks for the snack, by the way."

"You looked…hungry when you got here. I had no idea why, but now things are making some sense."

"I skipped dinner, too, you know."

"There's more to it than that." Cade tapped a finger

against his chin. "You know what I think you need?"

"If you say, 'to get drunk,' don't bother. My gramps already tried that."

Cade's face lit up in a big smile. "I've missed that old man. He good?"

A pang of guilt hit Kyle in the chest. Why had he pushed Cade away? To make himself into something he wasn't? What kind of douche did that? He huffed out a breath—the same kind of douche who dropped a girl for the same reason. "He's great."

"Excellent." Cade settled back against the leather couch, where the two of them had watched superhero movies and played video games for hours in another life. Today, he was wearing an *Arrow* T-shirt and plaid shorts that clashed magnificently with both the shirt and his carrot-red hair. Yet Kyle knew Cade was the only guy comfortable enough in his own skin to dress this way. Unlike him.

"You were saying something about what I need?" Kyle said. "You know I have to remind you because you never finish a thought, man."

Cade laughed. "True that. Okay, what you need is to try to get back together with Faith. Like, really try. Let nature take its course."

"Oh, is it that easy? I'll rush right out and try that," Kyle muttered. "News flash—not going to happen. I've lied to her and *everyone else* for four years. Plus her ex hates me and he's already making her life harder because of it. We stay together, he'll keep it up. I'm the worst thing that could ever happen to her."

"That's bullshit, and the fear talking. You know it, I know it." Cade stood abruptly. "Let's go to my room."

"On the first date? I'm flattered."

Cade waggled an eyebrow. "Ha, you should be."

"Oh, really?" He followed Cade down a hallway full of

framed photos. A six-year-old Kyle peeked out of a fort next to Cade. A nine-year-old Kyle beamed with Cade in front of a comic book store. A thirteen-year-old Kyle hunched his shoulders and stared blankly, while Cade held up a fish in triumph on his dad's fishing boat.

That's when it had all changed.

Shaking off his dark mood, he went into Cade's room. Aside from a plain blue bedspread replacing the *Iron Man* comforter on his bed, it wasn't much different. Sure, the posters had gone from *Dragon Ball Z* to manga and high-concept Marvel comic drawings, but the room was totally Cade.

"Sit." Cade pointed at a chair by his desk, then shut his bedroom door.

"You aren't going to steal my virtue, are you?" Kyle asked.

"You wish." Cade went to his nightstand and pulled out a book without letting Kyle see the cover. "Now, this might surprise you, but I've slept with three girls. Three, Kyle. And all of them told me they enjoyed it. One went so far as to say I was, how'd she put it? 'Very generous with both my hands and my time.'"

Kyle's eyebrows raced for his hairline. "Are you shitting me? God, *you're* the real player of Suttonville High. Jesus, man."

Cade smirked. "Come to think of it, one of them called on Jesus a few times."

Holy hell. Kyle dropped his face into his hands. "If you're trying to make me feel better, it's not working. If anything, I feel worse."

"That's not why I told you." Cade sat on the foot of his bed and kicked Kyle's ankle. "Look at me, young padawan. Teach you the ways of the Force, I will."

"I don't think Yoda read the *Kama Sutra*, dumbass." But he laughed. "So what are we really doing?"

"I'm providing you with free psychotherapy, if you'd just shut up."

Kyle shook his head, rolling his eyes to the ceiling. "Just because your mom is a psychologist doesn't mean you're qualified to mess with my brain."

"I'm taking college-level psychology at UTA this semester," Cade said softly. "And my mom's been helping me with case studies. I might be more qualified than you think."

Shit. One more thing he didn't know about Cade. He was such an asshole, and the only way to stop being an asshole was to stop being an asshole. Kyle sat up straighter. "Okay, let's hear it."

"You lost your mom early," Cade said. "So you've always been a little wary of girls because you had no familial exposure to them. You always shied away from the girls chasing you on the playground in fourth grade at Summit, while I was trying desperately to let them catch me. On the rare occasion that they bothered to chase me at all." He chuckled. "By the time we were in middle school, I thought you might be gay, because you looked uncomfortable with everyone and everything, and I wanted to tell you it would all be okay, but you quit talking to me. Then all these rumors started in high school and I decided maybe you were overcompensating for being overlooked before. A late bloomer maybe."

"This is pretty damn embarrassing to hear, you know," Kyle said frankly.

"I'm not judging. Get that through your head—I don't judge you. I never have." Cade glared at him. "I'm your friend. You may've stopped being mine for a while, but I didn't."

TKO to the guy in the Arrow *T-shirt.* Kyle stared at his hands. He'd done so many things wrong. Now, maybe, he could get some things right. "I'm sorry. Really. I should've been...better. At everything."

"I don't blame you one bit for morphing into 'Kyle Sawyer,

bad-boy wonder. King of the hoodies, duke of badassery.' You had your reasons, and they were logical. Painfully understandable, to be honest." Cade shrugged. "Besides, I figured you'd remember the real you at some point and come back. Shall we continue?"

"Oh, what the hell. Sure."

"So now you've built all of this—meaning girls and relationships and sex—up in your head until it's an *Event*, capital *E*. You're scared to fail because you've been taught—cruelly—that failure leads to humiliation. That being sensitive, smaller than other guys, and dyslexic made you a target. Even though a lot of that's changed, you're still afraid to be hurt, so you either avoid relationships, or you end them before you can get your heart broken."

Now it was Kyle's turn to let his mouth hang open. "So you're saying my hang-ups are Cameron's fault?"

"And all the other bullies. And your teachers, not having your mom, and always being told to suck it up by your dad and your grandpa. I really do like that old man, but he's pretty old-school. His solution to all this hurt you in the long run. Turning you into something you aren't isn't the best way to solve problems even if it protected you from the worst school had to offer."

Kyle slumped in his chair, too tired to ask his bones to hold him upright. "Jesus."

"So I've been told." Cade whacked him on the knee. "Now, for your cure."

"Can't wait," he mumbled.

"First, think about what scares you. When you started having doubts last night, what happened?"

"Faith…" He clenched his hands together. "Faith seems to want more than just revenge. Like a relationship, and she probably thinks I have that stuff down. Thing is, I'm pretty sure she's a virgin, too, but she thinks I'm this great…this great…"

"Lover," Cade said. "If you can't say it, you can't do it, man."

"Jesus."

"You keep saying that. I think that means He wants me to help you."

"Okay, fine. Lover. There, I said it." Kyle closed his eyes. Was it hot in here?

"Easy, take a breath. You're *fine*, Kyle." Cade tapped him on the ankle with his foot again. "Open those eyes. There's no girl here to scare you."

Kyle did as he was asked, pinning Cade with a hard glare. "I'm not afraid of girls."

Cade clapped his hands. "A breakthrough! Outstanding."

"You want me to be pissed with you?"

"Yes." Cade leaned forward, his expression intense. "Because, man, you are one angry son of a bitch. It's seeping out of your pores."

Kyle clenched his fists. There wasn't anything to hit, though. "Of course I'm angry. I'm an eighteen-year-old virgin who hides behind a costume to keep from feeling like hell all day long."

"And how well do you think a pissed-at-the-world guy can let go and enjoy sexy times with a gorgeous lady, huh? No, wait, I'll tell you." Cade jabbed a finger at him. "*Never.* That's your problem. You're still so damned hurt that you can't even see that people outside your house care about you. You think that you have to be *someone else* to be worth knowing."

Kyle let out a shaking breath. "That hurt, man."

"Good. You're not going to deal with this unless it hurts." Cade stood and started pacing. "Kyle, you forgot who you are. You shoved away everything you enjoy to hide behind a suit of armor that's choking you day in and day out. I know baseball makes you happy. And gardening does, too. But how many people at school know you have a lawn business?"

"You and Faith," he mumbled. "Oh, and Faith's friend Violet."

"And why's that?"

Kyle's neck, face, and chest burned. "Because I'm too embarrassed to tell anyone."

"Why?" Cade's tone was hard, giving him no quarter, no way out.

"Because I'm worried someone will give me crap about it. That it's weird, or something. Like it's beneath them, and I'm too stupid to get a 'real job.'"

"Not worried," Cade said, still harsh, still pushing just like a coach would. "*Scared*. Say it. Say it and own it, then check how you feel."

Kyle jumped up to face him, all the frustration pouring out of him at once. "I *am* scared, you jackass. Okay? I'm terrified."

Cade patted his shoulder awkwardly. "I know. But here's a secret—so is everyone else. You're pretty awesome, man. Good-looking, athletic, rich as hell, and despite all those character flaws, a nice guy. Don't let someone else's opinion shit on that for you." One corner of Cade's mouth lifted in a sad smile. "I'm goofy, a complete nerd, and totally middle class. But I'll tell you something—I'm willing to trust that other people won't be douches about all my shortcomings and like me for me. And that, my friend, is why I'm good in the sack."

"Because you're goofy and totally middle class?" Kyle asked, finding a sad smile of his own. Hadn't Faith said almost the same thing, about everyone having baggage?

"No, because I trust people. And I work hard to make sure they can trust me. You've made a good step that direction, coming to see me about this. Next step will be to try to fix things with Faith. She'll understand if you give her a chance."

"I hurt her pretty bad."

"Girls are resilient. And another word of wisdom? It's always the quiet ones. Those girls? I'm telling you, they're the best. Don't go for the flirty, bold ones. They're too into themselves. Sweet girls, given the right care and feeding, will blow your mind."

Kyle laughed uncomfortably. "I feel really weird about this conversation."

"As you should." Cade picked the book up off his bed. "Sex manual. My mom gives it to clients who have intimacy issues. I know you know how the mechanics work, but this will help with other stuff. Oh, and Kyle? You need to buy some condoms. That way you don't have an excuse to back out when you're finally ready."

Shaking his head, Kyle took the book. Half the words rearranged themselves on the page. Good thing there were pictures, because he was pretty sure his reading tutors wouldn't help him decipher these pages. "If my grandpa finds this, he'll give me hell for a month."

"No, he won't. Remember—trust people not to be douches. Vulnerability is a good thing. Girls find it pretty sexy, my man."

Kyle tucked the book under his arm, careful not to look at the cover. "This is the weirdest conversation I've ever had."

"But do you feel better?" Cade's expression was hopeful.

Kyle thought it over. For once, starting a relationship with Faith—even kissing her, and maybe more—didn't make him feel all spastic inside. Maybe she'd understand why he did the things he'd done to survive high school. Maybe she wouldn't laugh, or get pissed. "Yeah. Funny enough, I do."

"Good." He beamed. "That'll be eight hundred dollars."

"Ha-ha. How about a burger sometime this week?"

"Can't. I'm running sound for the musical. We perform in two weeks, so I have rehearsal all the freaking time. How about next Sunday?"

He gave Cade a fist bump. "Sunday's good."

He started to go, but Cade stopped him. "Are you going to the musical?"

Good question. "Not sure."

"I think you should. She'd want you there. Really."

Kyle nodded and headed downstairs and out to his car. After he climbed in, he sat for a minute, letting his thoughts settle. He caught sight of the box Mrs. Gladwell had given him. He'd shoved it in the backseat on Saturday, and hadn't opened it. Cade's tough talk about trust and fear convinced him to stop avoiding it.

He pulled off the lid. Inside was a bunch of candy.

And a ticket to the musical on opening night.

When he got home, he went into the living room, feeling bruised all over. Whoever said mental pain doesn't hurt as bad as physical pain was an idiot. He flopped on the couch, his brain too scrambled to settle down. Cade had warned him— he had to be hurt to get better.

He'd been sitting there for twenty minutes before Grandpa came to find him.

"What's got your goat?"

Kyle stared into the gas fireplace in their living room, still in his workout gear. "Nothing."

"Bullshit, kid." Grandpa flopped onto the leather couch next to him. "You're practically comatose. And I hate to break it to you, but you smell like a yak."

Kyle didn't even crack a smile. "You don't know what a yak smells like."

"I was stationed in Vietnam for two years. I know a yak when I smell one."

Kyle closed his eyes and counted to ten. Sometimes

that was the only way to deal with the old man. "Fine. I had another blowup with Faith earlier. I keep screwing things up."

Plastic rustled and Grandpa handed him an Oreo. "Eat that. You'll feel better."

"This is a bribe."

"Damn right. And I have more. I'll give you the whole package if you move of your own volition."

"I'm just feeling messed up is all." Kyle ate the Oreo even though he wasn't hungry. "I went to Cade's. He gave me some advice. About Faith mostly, but about other stuff, too."

"He's a smart kid. You gonna listen?" Grandpa asked.

It took him a minute, but Kyle nodded. "I'm beat. I think I'll go to bed."

"Good plan." Grandpa stood and brushed the Oreo crumbs off his lap onto the good Persian rug.

"Rosanna's going to kill you."

"She won't have a chance." He grinned. "I asked Maven to go to San Antonio with me. We're leaving tomorrow. There's a Kansas reunion tour going through there Wednesday night, and I bought front-row seats, thought we'd make a trip of it. That's why I need you to start moving, so I don't have worry about you being alone for a few days."

Kyle jerked in surprise. "Alone? Where's Dad?"

"He's leaving for Chicago, first thing. Some board meeting." Grandpa's expression turned shrewd. "You'll have the place to yourself until Friday afternoon. Use that time to get right with yourself, kid."

Grandpa gave him a bracing pat on the shoulder and wandered back toward his den, whistling "Carry on Wayward Son."

Kyle sank back against the couch. Could he do this? Could he patch things up with Faith? He wanted to, and he knew what it was going to take. At some point, he had to figure this out, and right now seemed like a pretty good time, given the carnage of the last few days.

He'd do anything to erase Faith's hurt expression from his brain and replace it with a memory of her smile. A plan started to form in his mind, but he was going to need some help.

Time to see if he could actually let himself trust.

He fished his phone out of his pocket and dialed Cade, who answered with a barrage of cursing that left Kyle impressed. "You kiss your mother with that mouth?"

"Kyle? Shit, I thought you were someone else."

Kyle frowned. "Someone giving you trouble?"

"Oh, some jackass on the debate team, talking smack. Keeps calling me, and I was too pissed to check caller ID before letting loose." Cade made an annoyed sound. "It's only been an hour. Already having second thoughts?"

"No." He scooted to the edge of the couch, ready to stand and face what was in front of him. "What time is rehearsal tomorrow?"

"Five thirty. We're working on the nightmare scene. Why?"

"I might need your help with something." His game started at five. This was going to take some work. "The nightmare scene...as in Laurey's nightmare? Or as in 'it's a nightmare working on this scene'?"

"Both."

"Thanks."

"For what?"

Kyle stood and stretched. He had some things to do before bed. "For everything."

The next morning, Kyle left for school early after Dad gave him the "no parties, young man" lecture, and Grandpa gave him a hundred bucks. "For pizza," he said.

"For an army?" Kyle asked.

"I know how you eat," Grandpa retorted.

Once at Suttonville, he looked for Cameron's car. Not here yet. Fine, whatever. He'd find him at some point. They had some business to take care of—the sooner, the better.

Still, the morning wasn't without surprises. He went to his locker, and there was Violet, leaning against it, her purple hair gleaming and her stare like dark bullets.

"You can go to hell, Kyle Sawyer," Violet growled. "*No one* hurts my best friend and gets away with it."

He hunched his shoulders inside his letter jacket. It was the first time he'd worn it, rather than his trusty hoodie, but it was flimsy protection against a girl who was part rabid fairy and part ninja. "I'm glad you're here. I was planning to find you later."

Violet stomped her foot. "You're supposed to argue with me. I want a fight this morning."

"Sorry. I only have one fight on my mind and it's with someone a lot taller than you."

She made a sound low in her throat, like a cat about to claw his eyes out. "I'm tall enough."

"I don't doubt that. You're pretty terrifying, and I'm being sincere." He leaned against the lockers next to her. "I need your help."

"Why on this heavenly blue planet would I *ever* help you?"

"For Faith. I need to make things right with her, and I plan to go big. You in?"

All the air went out of her sails, and her quivering rage went with it. "Well, when you put it that way. What's cooking, big boy?"

"Can you show up toward the end of play rehearsal? Cade said they'll be done around seven thirty, and he'll have something for you to do on my behalf."

"And what's that?" she asked, tilting her head. "Please tell me it's something illegal. I really want it to be illegal."

"Wow, you are a little monster." He smiled down at her. "I'm so tempted to pat you on the head right now."

"Do it and lose a testicle."

"I believe you, and no. Nothing illegal." He laughed when Violet let out a disappointed sigh. "I need you to give Faith something, that's all."

She blew out a breath that made her bangs flutter. "Fine. You have my number. Tell this Cade guy to text me when the operation, or whatever, is a go."

Kyle stuck out his right hand. "Shake on it?"

She gave his hand a suspicious look. "I don't know where that hand's been."

"Caressing the steering wheel of a year-old Charger."

She lunged forward and gripped his hand. "Ooh, I can almost feel the engine purring. My payment for helping you with this is the chance to drive that beast on a deserted road."

"Deal."

Kyle left her feeling a little more hopeful.

He felt even more charged up when he spotted Cameron walking down senior hall alone. It was time to do something he should've done four years ago. It was time to let go of everything that scared him, and Cameron was all of that personified. After today, the only fear left would be whether or not Faith decided to give him a chance.

Whether or not he could gut out his nerves and take that chance would be a bridge to cross later.

Kyle followed Cameron until they were in front of an empty classroom, then he grabbed him by the back of his letter jacket and dragged him through the door.

"What the complete fuck!" Cameron yelled, trying to turn around to see who it was, but Kyle grabbed one of his arms and wrenched it behind his back.

He frog-marched Cameron to the corner of the room so they were hidden behind a file cabinet and slammed him against the wall. "I have one thing to say, and you better listen. Leave Faith alone. You want to come after me? Do it. But leave her alone. Tell your friends to lay off, or I'll take batting practice against your balls. Are we clear?"

He gave Cameron's arm a yank to emphasize what he said. Cameron hissed with pain. "Sawyer, I'm going to kick your ass. You know it and I know it."

"Not this time, dickweed. I'm an inch taller and twenty-five pounds of muscle heavier. I'm not that short, scared kid you bullied and pissed on in eighth grade. You come after me again, you'll end up in pain. You mess with Faith and I'll need bail, as God is my witness."

Cameron struggled, and Kyle yanked on his arm again. "I'm not kidding. We're done, or you'll be sorry you ever screwed with me."

"Fine." Cameron's voice was shaking. "Fine! I won't bug Faith again. I'll tell the other guys not to even look at her."

Kyle released him and took a step back. "I'll be watching to make sure you do."

Cameron shot him a look of pure loathing. "You better watch your back, Sawyer. I'll leave Faith alone, but you're fair game, asshole. This doesn't change anything."

A cold smile spread over Kyle's face. "You're wrong. It changes *everything.*"

Kyle trotted around the bases, to the cheers of his team. Homered at his first at bat. That made what he was about to do a little more palatable. Besides, it was someone else's turn to shine.

Coach gave him a swat as he jogged into the dugout. "Not bad, Sawyer."

"Thanks." He accepted the high fives of his team before sneaking over to check his phone. Cade texted—he *texted*—to let Kyle know it was almost time. Okay, this was it. He might be thrown off the team for this, but some things were worth the cost.

He swallowed hard and went to Coach's side. "Coach, I hate to do this, and I wouldn't if it wasn't important, but there's someplace I need to be."

Coach frowned. "We're in the bottom of the second."

"I know, and I swear I wouldn't ask, but…I'm needed somewhere else."

Coach's frown deepened. "Is this about a girl?"

Kyle hid a wince. "Please, sir. Ledecky deserves a shot. He's your future, and we're up five to two. Give him a chance. I promise I'll stay late every practice for the rest of the season. Just give me this one thing."

Ledecky had perked up at the sound of his name. "I can do it, Coach. Give me a chance."

Coach looked entirely bewildered, both eyebrows raised. The team started cheering around them and Kyle turned. Tristan had just hit a two-run shot. "We're up by seven to two now. You don't need me tonight."

Finally, Coach relented. "Fine, okay. I don't even want to know, but if you miss a single practice or game the rest of the season, I'll bench you for the remainder."

Kyle grinned in relief. "Fair enough. Thank you, sir."

He ran to his car, dusted the dirt off his baseball pants, and drove over to the theater. So maybe the old man was right and he did smell like a yak, but he didn't have any time to spare.

Violet was waiting at the front door, and she waved him in. "Hello, holy shoulders," she stage-whispered, looking him over. "Nice look. I like the cleats."

A blush crept up his neck. That girl's gaze was like an MRI. "Have they started?"

"Yeah. Josh is already whining, and he dropped her on the first little lift." Violet's eyes narrowed. "He's such a little diva. He didn't even apologize. But I digress. You have a date."

Kyle nodded and sneaked through the doors at the back of the theater to let his eyes adjust to the dark. Cade gave him a thumbs-up from the sound booth a few seats over.

On the stage, a crowd had gathered. There were a number of chorus dancers, and the kid with the boots must be Josh. Faith stood center stage, dressed in her fluffy skirt, a different leotard, and her ballet slippers. Even from here, he could see the bright spots of frustration standing out on her cheeks.

"Remember," Cade whispered. "Knight in shining armor."

"I'm fine." And he was. All day long, he'd tested himself. After confronting Cameron, his confidence had grown each passing hour. He'd even managed a quick smile Faith's direction during lunch. The fact that she'd looked away didn't bother him in the least. He had a good feeling he could change her mind.

"Seriously, please tell me we're redoing this. I can't lift her," Josh called to the director, who was sitting in the fifth row. "Sorry."

"Joshua, enough." The director waved his clipboard in frustration. "Faith, I'm so sorry. Unless I can find a stunt double in the next five minutes, we'll have to redo the whole scene."

"That's your cue." Cade pushed a button and the music started back up.

The director turned around, looking annoyed, then confused as Kyle jogged past him. Holding his nerves in check, he sprang up on the stage in one jump, ignoring the stairs entirely. "Is this where I try out for stunt double?"

The clipboard clattered to the floor. "Who are you? And why are you wearing cleats on my stage?"

Kyle stood tall next to Faith at center stage. "I'm the guy who can lift Laurey over my head."

Faith's mouth was hanging open. "Kyle, what are you doing?"

He winked at her and turned back to the director. "What do you say? Can I audition?"

"I'll restart the music!" Cade called, without waiting for an answer.

Kyle turned to Faith. "I know what two of the lifts are. What's the third?"

"Just lift me straight up by my waist, no turn." She sounded bewildered, but pleased. Good enough. "I'll cue you."

He rolled his shoulders. "Let's do it."

Her eyes sparkled. "Remember, you asked for this."

The music swelled and Faith twirled around, straight into his open arms. "Straight up."

He grabbed her waist and lifted, until his arms were over his head. Faith squealed, and he brought her down.

"That was *high*. Okay, next move. Over there." She pointed to stage right, whirling away from him. "Lift from last week."

"I'm on it." He trotted over to stage right, ignoring the delighted stares from the chorus girls and the pissy look on Josh's face.

Faith danced all around the stage, her face crumpled in despair. He almost believed it, except for the twitch of a smile at the corner of her mouth. She turned back his direction, spinning so that her back was to him. Her knees bent, and he grabbed her hips. She leaped, and he turned her in a circle as she held that bent-legged pose, just like before. Her form was beautiful, and one of the chorus girls breathed, "Wow."

"Last one," Faith said. "I'll be back."

"I'll be here!"

"No!" The chorus girl next to him pointed at center stage. "There, quick!"

He jumped over just as Faith spun toward him. He caught her waist, then her thigh. "We're going all the way."

"I bet you say that to all the girls," she said as he lifted her from the floor.

He almost dropped her, but pulled it together, and dipped her head like yesterday. Then, to show Josh what a real man looked like, he lifted her straight up, until his arms were fully extended. Tightening his core, he balanced her all the way around as he turned.

"Holy. Shit!" a chorus girl crowed.

"Damn," another agreed. "I want a turn!"

Kyle set Faith down slowly, gently, until her front foot was balanced, and let her go.

She was breathing hard, and her cheeks were red, but her smile stretched ear to ear. "You are the craziest guy in the entire world. And that was *amazing.*"

Kyle turned to the director, bowed at the waist, then ran and jumped off the stage. A couple of girls in the violin section in the orchestra pit cheered. He blew Faith a kiss and ran back up the aisle.

"Wait! Where are you going?" the director was yelling. "You got the job!"

Kyle let out a loud whoop and flung himself through the doors and out of the theater, feeling like himself for the first time in four long years.

Chapter Thirty-Five

"But he can't sing!" Josh was protesting. "How can he have the part?"

"He doesn't, dummy," Alyssa snapped. "Didn't you hear Mr. Fisk? He's your stunt double for the nightmare scene. That's all."

Samuel, who had the male lead as Curly, nodded in agreement. "Take it like a man, Josh. Sawyer is a natural, and he has arms like a Greek god." He grinned at Faith. "Too bad he's straight."

"Enough, enough!" Mr. Fisk pinched the bridge of his nose. "Faith, would you please ask him if he'll do it? We can teach him his dance steps pretty easily. An athlete with quick feet like that will pick it up just fine. I don't want him lifting you over his head for the performance, though. Too much liability. The fish lift with a dip is enough."

Faith shivered, thinking about it. She'd been so high up, she could see the crowns of every head on stage. It hadn't scared her one bit—Kyle would never drop her. She almost squealed in delight just remembering it. "I'll talk to him about it. If the performances don't conflict with baseball, I think he'll say yes."

Mr. Fisk nodded. "Good. Now, I've had enough excitement for one evening. That's a wrap. See everyone tomorrow."

Faith took off backstage on wobbly legs to change into her flip-flops. She couldn't believe Kyle had come, and that whole rushing in to save the day when Josh dropped her? She could kiss him until one of them fainted for that.

She had to find him first, though. Where had he gone? He'd taken off, laughing like crazy, and disappeared.

"Gazelle, dahling?" Vi stepped around the curtain. She was carrying a large bouquet. "I have something for you."

"Oh, you shouldn't have!" Faith said, smiling at the roses. They were gorgeous—blood red and just starting to open. The arrangement was perfect, too, with greenery and baby's breath expertly placed inside the bouquet, like the expensive arrangements Dad bought Mom on their anniversary.

"Ha, these aren't from me." Vi held up a single carnation wrapped in crumpled green tissue paper. "This is mine. I was saving it for the performance, but I couldn't let someone else give you flowers first."

Faith laughed. "Okay, you *really* shouldn't have. But who are the roses from?"

Vi smirked. "Give you one guess. If he hadn't looked like a sad puppy when he asked me for help, I would've trashed the flowers, but he made me promise to give them to you. After all that just now, I'm glad I relented. He really put on a show out there."

Faith's eyes unfocused as she thought about the feel of his hands on her waist. "Yeah, he sure did."

"Hey!" Violet gave her a little shove. "Back to earth now, tiny dancer. Take your flowers."

Faith snorted. "Is there a note?"

Violet handed the bouquet to her. "Yes. Be proud of me—I was good and didn't read it."

"I'm very proud." Chuckling, Faith opened the envelope tucked inside the bouquet. It was too big for a flower arrangement, and heavy. He'd used good stationery. Where did a high school boy find stationery? Her hands shook as she opened the envelope, finding a long note written in Kyle's cramped handwriting, with a few words scratched out:

Faith,

You have every single reason to hate me. But I need to ~~explan~~ explain. I didn't push you away because I wanted to hurt you, but because I was ~~sacred~~ scared. You probably already know I'm a guy with secrets, but what you don't know is just how big they are. For the first time, though, I want someone to know me—the real me. If you're willing to hear me out, meet me in the back parking lot after ~~rehersal~~ rehearsal. We'll go for a drive and I'll tell you everything I was too scared to say before.

Please.

Kyle

She tucked the envelope into her bag. It felt heavy, hanging there with the weight of what he said. Was she ready for this? After everything, was he really going to let her in on his secrets?

"Well?" Vi asked. "Don't leave me on a cliffhanger."

"He wants to see me," she said. "Now."

"I thought he might. Are you going to go?"

Faith smiled. "I think I should, don't you?"

"If you don't," Alyssa said, coming up behind them, "I'll go. Seriously, you don't leave a guy like that waiting."

No, you didn't. She gathered up her things. "Vi, I'm going to tell my mom I'm out with you. Cover for me?"

"You know me—I love a good intrigue." Violet held up a

bag. "I already told your mom we were going out tonight and stopped by to grab some extra clothes for you."

"One step ahead, as usual." Faith smiled. "What, you don't think I should go out there in a leotard?"

"I'd go out there naked," Alyssa muttered.

"*Thank* you for your opinion." Vi jiggled her fingers at her. "Bye now."

Alyssa grumbled, but took off without argument. Faith shook her head. "What's really going on?"

Violet shrugged. "Honestly, I don't know. But he's made it into a really big deal, so I wanted you to be prepared. I brought you a maxi dress and a sweater. Not too dressy, not a leotard and a poufy skirt."

"Good point." Faith took the clothes into the dressing room and changed. Her skin tingled with nerves, and she didn't look at herself in the mirror. She wasn't sure she could bear to see the hope on her face. She'd been hurt too many times in the last ten days. Proceed with caution—that had to be her new motto.

She came out and found that Violet had left. Rolling her eyes at all the clandestine behavior, she waved good-bye to the stragglers still left and let herself out the stage door to the parking lot.

Kyle stood waiting next to his pickup truck. He must've run home because he'd changed into a button-down, jeans, and his Sperrys. Some things never changed, though: he was hotter than hell, and the way he was looking at her made her legs feel weak.

Faith wanted to walk to him, but nerves—and fear—kept her glued to the back door. What would he tell her? What would change between them? Would he stay this time?

He smiled at her, this slow, sexy thing that set her heart on fire. Screw fear. She had somewhere to be.

She hauled her dance bag higher up on her shoulder

and smoothed the wrinkles out of her dress before starting across the parking lot. He took a step forward and opened the passenger door as soon as she made it to the car.

"You came," he said, sounding surprised. "I wasn't sure you would, after…everything."

"I like a good secret," she murmured, staring down at the asphalt, embarrassed and nervous after seeing the spark of fear and hope in his own eyes. "And I like a guy not afraid to dance."

He took her bag and waited for her to climb into the truck before closing her door and walking around. When he slid behind the wheel, he stared straight ahead. "Are you sure you're okay going somewhere with me?"

"Yes," she said softly.

He swallowed. "Because, uh, I thought the best place to go would be my house. I don't, um, I don't really take people there. It might help you understand some things."

She wanted to ask him why now, and why her, but she nodded. "Okay."

"Before we go, though, I feel like I need to tell you nobody's home." He glanced quickly at her, then looked away. "My grandpa's in San Antonio with his lady friend, and my dad left this morning to go to Chicago for a board meeting. They're both gone until Friday. If you aren't okay with going home with me, I understand."

She knew what he was saying—he was worried she was scared to be alone with him—but she couldn't be. This Kyle wasn't someone she was afraid to be alone with. "That's fine."

He nodded, a jerky movement with too much force behind it, and started the truck. They drove in silence through town, until she asked, "Where's the Charger?"

"First secret already, huh?" He laughed softly. "The Charger was given to me. It was my birthday present from Grandpa when I turned seventeen last year. The truck is mine. I bought it with my own money, and I love it. I thought the best way to start off my trek to honesty was to pick you up in the Toyota."

Faith looked at the worn upholstery, the broken radio, the door handle that jiggled as they drove, and a little bit of warmth stole through her chest. He had the coolest car in the whole senior class, but he loved an ancient truck because he bought it himself. She blinked fast to push back the tears threatening to brim on her lashes. "It's a good secret. And I like the truck, too. It's good for hauling azaleas."

"It is."

He drove her to the north side of town, and Faith's pulse sped up. The neighborhoods out here were far wealthier than her own, and her family was quite well off. Hell, these people were wealthier than Violet's family, and they had lakefront property. "Why are we in The Hills?"

Kyle sighed. "Secret number two."

He pulled onto a side street that was bordered by trees. Like the road to Violet's, their branches created a canopy overhead. The setting sun glowed through the leaves. The street wound up a low hill and ended at a gate.

Kyle pushed a button on a garage door opener clipped to his sun visor, and the gate pulled back. Behind it was one of the biggest houses she'd ever seen. It had to be at least ten thousand square feet. Made out of dark brick, its two-story front had ivy climbing one wall, and huge picture windows overlooking a riotous front garden. A circle drive curved around front, but Kyle took the second driveway that led behind the house to a six-car garage. Trees grew all over the yard back here, too. Between their branches, she could just make out a large covered patio and a hint of a pool.

"*This* is your house?" Faith's eyes hurt from being open so wide. "I mean, I knew you had money, with the car and all, but I thought your family was more like mine."

"Yes, this is my house." He sounded tired and teasing at the same time. "You're riding in a landscaping truck with a trust-fund gardener."

Faith covered her mouth and laughed helplessly into her hands. "Oh my God. I can see why you don't tell people. You wouldn't know who liked you for you and who liked you for…"

She trailed off awkwardly, but he nodded. "For the money. Yeah. My dad always asks why I don't bring many people home, but Grandpa knows, and goes along with it."

"Okay, if these are only the first few secrets, what are the rest?"

He parked in front of the garage and came around to open her door. "Come in and I'll explain everything."

They entered the house through what he called the mudroom and she called a damn enormous laundry and storage area. You could play soccer across the floor and not hit anything end to end.

"This is the kitchen," he said, going through the next door. "We spend a lot of time in here."

"Who's 'we'?" she asked. "Your grandpa, your dad. Anyone else?"

"Rosanna's here a lot, but she doesn't live here." He paused. "She's, uh, our housekeeper. She takes care of us because, as she put it, 'Three men, living alone? You boys would live on hamburgers without me.'"

He said the quote in a falsetto and a slight Hispanic accent. Faith grinned in delight. "She sounds awesome. How old were you when you lost your mom?"

"She died when I was three. She and my grandmother. They were in a car accident. After that, Grandpa decided to move in with us, and we've been together since." He shrugged. "I'd say I missed them, but I was too little to remember. So it's been just us. My dad owns an investment firm, and my grandpa used to own J. Sawyer furniture."

"Wait a minute. You're *that* Sawyer?" Faith's mouth dropped open. "Mom's been trying to talk Dad into buying one of those dining sets for years."

Kyle scuffed his shoe against the floor. "Yeah. They're a little pricey."

"But they're gorgeous. Wow," Faith breathed, turning in a circle. The kitchen was high end, and she had a feeling the whole house would be. She went to their kitchen table—a six-seater, handmade out of gleaming oak. "Did your grandpa make this?"

"It's one of his first. He made it for Grandma when he came home from Vietnam."

"Beautiful." She ran a hand along the wood. It was satiny with age and use. "Where's your room?"

He jumped. Literally jerked like she'd crossed a rug and shocked him with the static. "You know what, that was rude of me to ask. Never mind."

His expression was a war between uncomfortable and determined. Determined won. "No, it's fine. It's upstairs."

He led her through a butler's pantry into a living room with all leather furniture, dark wood floors, and the newest electronics on the market. "This room is *so* guy."

"Be thankful I'm not taking you into Grandpa's den. Total man cave."

She laughed as he took her to a large staircase in a formal foyer at the front of the house. A crystal chandelier hung down from the twenty-foot ceiling overhead. "Kyle, I have house envy."

"Is that a good thing?"

She made a face. "I'm not entirely sure."

Upstairs he led her down a hall with walls covered with pictures of a boy growing up. In the first few, a beautiful woman with dark hair and shining blue eyes held a toddler with a big smile. Later, though, they changed to sports pictures and family vacations deep sea fishing or camping. The line between the two was stark.

Tears pricked at the back of her eyes. How had this life been, without a mother to hold him on her lap when he skinned his knee? Or teach him what girls were really like? Is that what made him run so hot and cold?

He opened a door. "Here we are."

Faith peeked inside. "This is as big as my second story."

And it was. In the corner, under a slanted roof, was a bed with a navy bedspread. The headboard was carved out of the same oak as the dining table. Definitely handmade, probably also by his grandfather. A window seat was cut into the slanted wall. On the other side of the room was a desk, a couch, and an entertainment system that rivaled the one in her living room.

She patted Kyle's arm. "I'm so sorry you have to live in such squalor."

"I know." He nodded solemnly. "But I make do."

She slipped inside and went to the couch. He followed more slowly and didn't sit until she patted the seat next to her. "Okay, I'm here. What did you want to tell me?"

His knee started bouncing. "It's kind of hard to know where to start."

"Maybe the beginning?"

He nodded and took a deep breath. "That would be seventh grade, but we've talked about most of that. It really started in eighth grade, the worst year of my life."

"Eighth grade was hard for me, too," she said. "But what was awful about yours?"

"Cameron Zimmerman."

He said it with such bitterness that she leaned away, breath stolen from her lungs. Just how horrible *was* Cameron? "Worse than the stuff you've already told me?"

"More stupid middle school stuff," Kyle mumbled. "Not important."

God, guys were so buttoned-up sometimes. Especially *this* guy. "You can't say he made your life hell, then tell me it's not important." She put her hand on his. "You said you were going to tell me everything."

He closed his eyes a moment. "You didn't go to Perkins for middle school, did you?"

"No, I went to Rosewood."

"Well, if you'd gone to Perkins, you'd know. It's blown over for most people, but not for me."

His shoulders were hunched around his ears, and his expression had a tortured pinch to it. Faith reached out, slowly, and took his hand. "Whatever it is, I won't be shocked."

He laughed in an unfunny way. "Oh, I don't know about that."

She shook her head. He obviously needed to talk about this. "I won't."

His body went slack, like he was either giving up or giving in. Faith held completely still, gripping his hand so he had a lifeline. Finally, he said, "Like I said, it started in seventh grade. Cameron played on a different Little League team, and my team killed them every time. Cameron was a second baseman then, before he settled on football. One game, I had to slide. I came in hot, and he missed the tag, so I was safe. For some reason, that set him off. One insult too many from our team, I guess.

"He started with petty stuff. His friends pestered me, pulled nasty pranks." From the look on his face, Faith wondered just how nasty those pranks had been. "Made a fool of me in front of the girl I liked, taped my homework and tests all over the school like I told you, crap like that."

"But that's not all," Faith said, sure of it. "They cratered you at one point, didn't they?"

He nodded, looking away. "It was the week of baseball tryouts in eighth grade. Most of the guys at Perkins saw me as this shrimp—I was a *lot* shorter then—and someone to beat on. Cade and I were bullied all through middle school, not just by Cameron, but by everyone with a bone to pick. So by then, I was pretty worn down."

She squeezed his hand. "I'm so sorry."

"It's over now. You need to understand what happened, though. They all knew I had an arm on me, even then. They'd seen me play in Little League. So when I went out for the Perkins team…"

His voice cracked, and he paused. Faith edged closer to him, sensing his pain. It was so close to the surface, her own heart ached, and she didn't even know why he'd been hurt. "What happened?"

"For the first two days of camp, I smoked the guys trying out for outfielder. I outhit, outcaught, and outthrew every last one of them. Including Cameron. I made that jackass look like a fool. If you wonder why he only does football and track, *I'm* why." Kyle's face broke into a brittle smile. "King of the grass. That's what the assistant coach called me. And it pissed the jocks off. This shrimp, this *nothing*, coming in and blowing them all away."

He let out a deep breath. "Anyway, on the last day, the real tryout day, I went into the locker room to change. While I was in there, in my freaking underwear, Cameron and two of his buddies grabbed me. They taped my mouth shut and tied my hands behind my back. Then, before locking me in the broom closet, one pinned me against the wall while Cameron wrote 'loser' on my forehead with Sharpie." He shook his head, cheeks red. "Not the way I wanted to find out that Sharpie comes off skin with rubbing alcohol. Anyway, they'd waited late enough that all the coaches were already outside. No one heard me kicking the door. One of Cameron's friends came back to let me out after tryouts were over and almost everyone had gone."

Kyle's fist clenched around Faith's hand, but she didn't let go. She leaned against him. "What happened then?"

"They'd told the coach I changed my mind, saying that I'd said 'this public school ball was for pansies' and that I'd gone back to my select team." He turned to look at her, and the hurt in his eyes made tears well up in hers. "They'd also taken all my clothes. All of them. There I was, crying like an ass, Sharpie on my forehead, and I had nothing to wear. I had to hide from the coaches and call my grandpa to come get me. He wanted to tell the coaches what happened, but I just... couldn't. I was too embarrassed. How would the coaches like having a punching bag on the team, no matter how well he caught?"

"That is the meanest thing I've ever heard," Faith said, anger lighting a fire in her skin. God, Cameron was such a malicious little prick. Was she really that blind not to see it? She'd been with him for six months. He must've been careful not to show that part of himself. If she'd known, she would've left him much sooner. "I have half a mind to kick Cameron in the balls the next time I see him."

"It doesn't matter," Kyle said, heat coloring his tone. His face was frozen in a frown, and he kept bouncing his leg in a nervous tic. "Don't you get it? I let him win. I was too weak to stand up for what I wanted. If any of this happened to me now, I would've gone out to the field naked, not giving one shit. But he tormented me over and over. So when we got home that night, Grandpa and I talked about how to change things, and that's how Kyle Sawyer, delinquent badass, was born. Lucky for me, I grew five inches the summer between eighth and ninth grade. From there, it was easy. I started dressing in black tees and hoodies. Didn't give anyone the time of day. Picked up a skateboard, though that's pretty much for show, because

Coach would kill me if I got hurt. And I made damn sure to kick a sophomore bully's ass the very first week of high school—broke his nose and got in-school suspension. The fact that he started it was the only reason I wasn't expelled. Grandpa was proud as hell, but I didn't enjoy it. That guy's not me—it's a persona. So when I say I'm not who you think I am, I really mean it."

I knew it. I knew *it.* She bit back a smile. "Wait, are you saying you *aren't* a delinquent?"

"No." He slipped his hand out of hers. "I'm not anything you think I am. Except a liar. That, I excel at."

"So," she said, giving him a shrewd look. "You *don't* like working on lawns?"

"No, I like that. I love it, actually. Which no one would ever believe."

"And you don't love baseball?" she asked.

"No, I do, it's just—"

"And you don't love your truck more than your badass Charger?"

"Well, I love them both, but for different reasons...what are you doing?"

Faith gave his arm a bracing pat. "Wondering why you think I don't know you. The *real* you."

"But..." Now *he* was frowning.

"No buts. I *know* you."

"You're too smart for your own good, Faith," he grumbled.

She noticed how his knee had stopped bouncing. Confession really was good for the soul. "Well, I know the Charger's yours, so the badass car isn't a lie." She cocked her head. "Do you drag race?"

The corners of his mouth lifted. "Only when douches in tricked-out Hondas gun their engines."

"Well, who doesn't?" she said, and he laughed. "And given the huge house, I don't think you shoplift, either."

"Definitely not. Well, except for a candy bar in sixth grade. I ate it on the way to the register, and a friend dared me to walk out. I did." He turned to her and the smile grew. "I felt so guilty that I left a dollar next to the register the next day."

And there he was—the real Kyle. The guy who loved plants as much as people, who paid attention when she talked, who danced with her when her own partner wouldn't. The same boy who called her dad "sir" and made her mom laugh. The solid, quiet, sweet, hardworking boy no one really knew.

Except her.

"You're a big softy." Relieved to see him smile, she reached out and ran her fingers along his shoulder. "And the tattoo?"

His eyes fell half closed. "That's real."

"Show me," she whispered.

Kyle flushed and stared at the floor.

She reached down for the hem of his shirt and gave it a little tug. "Please?"

"You've already seen it," he mumbled.

He sounded so shy, which surprised her after all the shirtless gardening last week. It made her want to see that tattoo even more—to run her fingers along it and feel the muscles beneath. An ache filled her middle. It wasn't just the tattoo she wanted to see.

"I haven't seen it up close."

He raised his head and met her eyes. There was something uncertain, but hungry, scared, and longing in his gaze. And she knew, right then, what was making her ache, and why. Her heart stuttered. She'd been so scared to admit it, thinking he was the wrong guy at the wrong time, unable to understand why he kept pushing her away.

But he was also the boy who saved her at rehearsal. Who took her to the arboretum for a date. Who made her crazy, uncertain, excited, and joyful all at once. Mom had seen through his facade last week…and Faith's, too.

"Kyle?" She reached for his hands and pulled up him up so they were standing, facing each other. "You don't have to take off your shirt. But…" Her heart banged painfully in her chest. God, this was it, wasn't it? She finally found the one guy who could turn her life upside down in the most perfect way.

She cleared her throat. "It's just…I finally figured out you're the guy I've been looking for. Not the delinquent Kyle, but the guy who turned my backyard into something beautiful. The Kyle who danced with me and took me to see an azalea garden. And especially the Kyle who was hurt a few years ago, but bounced back. You might be embarrassed by all that, but I'm not. It's part of you, and I like who you are. And it's not the tattoo I want to see. It's you. I want to see you. All of you."

Chapter Thirty-Six

KYLE

Kyle's breath caught in his throat. The way Faith was looking at him—his heart galloped around his chest, fighting against its restraints. "What?"

She smiled, but there were tears in her eyes. "I bare my soul, and you ask, 'what?' Another girl might be upset by that, but I'm too happy to care. Now, listen closely. You listening?"

He nodded, too breathless to speak.

"Good." She smiled and laid a hand on his chest. "I think you're amazing on the inside—and the outside doesn't hurt, either." She let out a soft, breathy laugh. "I want to be with you. All the time. And I *want* you, too. Now, in a week, in a year, whenever you're ready—it doesn't matter, as long as it's with you."

This must be what being struck by lightning feels like. Because his body was electrified, fried from end to end, and begging for another hit. Was that jolt terror? Desire? Both? Neither?

Everything was so confused. "I, uh, okay."

She chuckled. "Look, last time I checked, you have a little more experience with this than I do. Isn't there supposed to be more kissing and less awkward conversation?"

His insides collapsed into a miserable cold ball of guilt. "That's just it."

She slipped her arms around his neck. "What's 'just it'?"

Her lips brushed his cheek when she spoke, and he shuddered. One more lie to add to the list. How many was too many? He was sure this had to be the last straw. Any minute now, she was going to get fed up and leave him. *This close* and it was going to be over. "That day I pushed you away, it's… I was scared. Scared that you'd find out and laugh, or be angry."

"Angry about what?"

He sighed. "There's one more secret. See, I haven't actually…been with any girls. Not one. Hell, you're the first girl I ever kissed."

Her eyes flew wide and she leaned away. His entire body turned to ice. Yep, misery complete—she was going to walk out and leave him. And he deserved it.

"Really? You're a virgin? *You?*"

He nodded and held himself stiff. If she wanted to walk out, he wouldn't make things hard for her. "That whole player thing? It's a lie. Just like everything else—a persona to save myself. I'm actually kind of awkward with girls, and I didn't want you to know. That's why I pushed you away. I was falling apart inside, feeling so guilty about all the lying, and I was scared you'd….I don't know. I was just scared."

"Scared," she murmured.

"Yeah. So I was a dick because I couldn't bring myself to admit it. I've been a mess to deal with, and I'm sorry. I understand why you might want to walk away, because I wasn't honest about anything."

She took in a tiny breath, her expression confused, a little line of pinched skin forming between her eyebrows. "Oh."

God, he didn't want to lose her, to end it this way. *Tell her. Just tell her before it's too late, even if you end up hurt.* "But, Faith…I want you to know I never meant to hurt you. Because, um, because no one else—except you—made me want to try to work through all my crazy. And maybe I'm not who you think I am, but that only makes me want to be with you more. Out of all the girls who've been interested, you're the only one I ever acted *real* around. You're the first, in everything. I just wanted to tell you that, before you go." He swallowed against the tide of despair rising in his throat. "Because I wanted you to be the first for this, too."

She held really still. "You mean that?"

"Yeah." He waited for her to go. "I mean it."

"I'm glad you told me." Her arms tightened around him. "Now we can be awkward first-timers together."

"What?" he asked. God, he was making *no* sense at all. His brain had misfired. Why wasn't she stomping away? He'd lied and lied. Why was she still here?

"Kyle, whatever you're thinking, it's the fear talking. And you shouldn't be afraid of us." Faith's tone was kind, but commanding. "Kiss me."

She wasn't going? She really wasn't? Joy lit a slow fire that burned outward from his heart to his limbs. Yeah, he was going to damn well kiss her. But first… "I want to say one more thing."

She rolled her eyes, but she was smiling, and it was so, so beautiful. "I'm starting to think you're stalling."

"No," he said, fast. "I just need to tell you the truth about one last thing."

She bit her lip, like she was trying to swallow her smile and be serious, but she couldn't manage it, and it was adorable. "Proceed."

Now he was smiling, too. "You make me a better person,

and there's no one else I'd rather be with. And that's the truth."

"Now that was worth waiting for," she whispered, going up on her toes, ever the ballerina, so their faces were even. "So…that kiss?"

He took her face in his hands. "That kiss."

Her eyes fell shut, but he kept his open. He wanted to see her face as their lips finally met, and the soft sigh, the sweetness of her expression, was so worth it.

He let his eyes close, too. His pulse hammered; his skin burned. Her body was so soft against his.

Eventually Faith dropped back down. He could feel her shaking, and imagined her knees wouldn't hold her up anymore. Their kiss broke and she stared up at him, her warm brown eyes reaching down to his soul, pulling it free from the earth to send him sailing into the sky.

She unbuttoned his shirt, and he shivered when her hands brushed against his stomach. "Is this okay?" she asked.

"Yes. I'm just a little nervous," he admitted, heat flooding his cheeks. "But…don't stop."

Her fingers worked his shirt off his shoulders. "I think it's sweet, the guy being nervous, but you can trust me, Kyle. I won't break your heart."

"I know." And he did know. She'd take care of his heart, and he'd take care of hers.

She laid his shirt on the couch, then walked around to trace the tattoo. "It's beautiful. What kind of bird is that?"

"A hawk," he said. He was having trouble breathing, and he couldn't make himself care. The feel of her fingers on his skin was giving him a contact high. "I've always loved them—they're strong for their size, and fierce. I needed that, to remind me."

She kissed his shoulder, and goose bumps rose in the spot her lips touched. "Well, I love it."

He spun around and pulled her against him, kissing her, drowning in her. "I love every part of you."

She nuzzled his neck. "How do you know? There are parts you haven't seen."

"I still love them." God, his heart was going to explode any second. "But I'd like to see them."

She took his hands and guided them to the skirt of her dress. His palms skimmed her thighs as he slid it up and over her head. All she wore underneath was a white bra and matching underwear, and he couldn't help but stare. Faith wrapped her arms around her middle. He wasn't sure if she was cold or shy, but he could fix both problems.

"You're beautiful, Faith. In every way possible." He stepped in close, feeling the softness of her skin against his. "You're sure?"

She pressed her forehead against his collarbone. "Completely."

"Then it's a good thing Cade talked me into buying condoms a few days ago."

Now she outright laughed. "Cade's a good friend."

"He is. But I don't want to talk about him right now." He slid his palms down her bare arms and took her hands in his. He breathed in the scent of her hair. It smelled like forever. "I don't want to talk at all."

She tilted her mouth up to his. "Neither do I."

Chapter Thirty-Seven

Scared. He said he was scared. He'd sounded so ashamed of that, but it was music to her ears. She'd been so wrong about him, in the best way possible. Here was someone not looking for easy prey, but for someone to lead him as much as he led her.

Faith let go of Kyle's hands and traced the lines of his biceps to his forearms. "You know, baseball players have the sexiest arms. Especially baseball players who can lift ballerinas up over their heads."

He growled softly, his mouth tracing kisses along her shoulder. "And ballerinas have great legs."

To prove his point, he reached down to stroke the outside of her thigh. She leaned into him, her breath quick and sharp in her lungs. One—or was it both?—of them was trembling, and his mouth crushed hers. He kept one hand on her lower back, and she arched against him. It lit her up inside, but still she wanted more, if he was ready. Would he be?

She splayed a hand on his chest and pushed him back a step. His eyes were unfocused and his hair was a wreck. And those jeans riding low on his hips made her blood race hot through her veins. God, what a beautiful mess he was. "You're overdressed."

He flushed. "So are you."

His voice was hoarse, and he swayed on his feet like he was struggling to stay upright. She'd have to make the first move—he was too far gone to do anything but follow her lead. She reached for his hand and tugged him toward the bed. They made it three steps before he pulled her back into his arms, almost as if he couldn't bear to let go, even for a second. Smiling against his mouth, she walked backward, pulling him along, until they finally made it.

She slid onto his bed, crooking her finger at him. Kyle bounded after her, his expression sweet and tense. She pulled him close, resting his head against her chest, and ran her fingers through his hair. He closed his eyes and leaned into her hand, like he was starved and her touch was the only thing to sustain him. Maybe it was.

Were things a little awkward? Sure, but it was endearing, the way they learned at their own pace. She loved the gentle way his hands found places that made her world dissolve into sparks, and how he gasped her name when she found her own favorite places on his body. She loved this promise they made, here, now. Just the two of them, in their own little universe.

His heart raced under her hands when he glided over her, and she knew this had been the right choice. He could give her so much more than anyone else, even if it had taken him a while to see it.

And in the end, the look of wonder, of astonished release, on his face was the last puzzle piece falling into place.

Chapter Thirty-Eight

KYLE

He wanted to keep his eyes open, but he was too knocked over to try too hard. Faith had curled up next to him with her head on his chest, her body warm and soft. He'd have to take her back to school for her car soon, but he couldn't think about that, not yet.

"You okay?" she murmured, her breath tickling his skin.

Okay? He felt like a goddamned superhero. A really tired, satisfied superhero, but if he could move, he bet he'd fly.

"More than," he rumbled, the words slow and sleepy. "You?"

"Oh, yeah." She propped herself on one elbow. Her hair had fallen down her back, and a strand of it was draped over her shoulder. "I'm happy I was the one. And that you were mine."

"I'm still a train wreck." He stretched, eyes open just enough to notice how Faith's gaze trailed down his body. "But I'm your train wreck, if you'll have me."

"I already *had* you." She laughed. "But if you're asking me to be yours for more than just today, then yes."

He rolled over, facing away from her, and punched his pillow a few times before lying back down. "Now this day is perfect. I better turn off the lights so I don't wake up and find out I'm dreaming."

She gave his shoulder a little shake. "Hey, hibernating bear, much as I hate it, I need to go home. Remember, I have an Olympic archer living in my house, probably wondering where I am."

He struggled to sit up, blinking. "But you'll come back tomorrow?"

She took his face in her hands and kissed him. "Try to stop me."

He sat in his car in the driveway after dropping Faith off. Going into the house seemed too much like an end, and he wanted this day to stretch out forever.

There were two texts on his phone when he finally pulled it out. The first was from Violet: *Good job, Sawyer.*

The second was from Tristan: *That crazy Ledecky scored two runs and made a diving catch to save a double. Good call, man.*

Kyle smiled in the dark. He'd known Ledecky had it in him. He owed that kid, big-time.

His phone rang, and he laughed. "Yes, Cade?"

"Whoa, you sound a lot less stressed out. What happened after you two left?"

Kyle climbed out of his car and stared up at the stars, unable to quell the crazy grin on his face. For the first time in a long while, he felt whole, and he owed that to Faith. "Everything, man. Everything."

Epilogue

She mock-screamed as Curly was killed by Jud at the start of the nightmare ballet. The stage went dark except for the spotlight on her, and she danced in mourning as the sets were moved behind her and the dancers ran into place. One of them, a cowboy with broad shoulders, arms straining at his sleeves and a brooding, stern expression on his face, stalked toward her, heralded by two mocking cancan girls.

Dear God, Kyle looked good in costume, and she had a really hard time keeping her expression terrified and grief-stricken.

True to Mr. Fisk's prediction, Kyle had picked up the dance steps in one practice. He hit his marks in time with the music without any trouble, and kept character perfectly.

She'd known he could pull it off—he'd already proven he was a consummate actor, with four long years of experience playing a part.

She whirled toward him, and he lifted her straight up in one fluid movement. A few members of the audience clapped.

He spun her around, pulling her close. Their eyes met, and his held a flicker of amusement as she leaned back like a rag doll, moving at his every whim.

He released her and she spun away, holding her head in her hands in fear as the chorus closed in on her again, forcing her back to Jud. The second lift went off perfectly, with Kyle's steady strength giving her balance she needed to hold her pose. Adrenaline shot through her veins—now it was only the fish lift. Time to blow minds and impress that agent in the audience who'd come to see her perform.

That was Kyle's doing, too.

She leaped and flew, pinballing around the chorus, driven to Jud like some horrible magnet. As she turned toward him, Kyle winked and she held her breath. Mr. Fisk was going to kill them later, but who cared?

She pirouetted into his arms, which came expertly around her waist and thigh. He lifted her, did the dip and whispered, "Here we go."

Then she was flying, sailing above his head and everyone else's. The audience whistled and applauded as Kyle set her down. It was so hard to keep the grin off her face.

Terrified, remember, you're terrified.

She danced and danced, letting the music and the moment sweep her up and in. It was perfect.

The chorus surrounded her, and she stumbled in pretend horror, a mute scream on her lips. She was unable to escape him, and Kyle grabbed her and hauled her over one shoulder. She pounded on his back, mock-kicking at him, as he carried her off stage. The curtain fell, and the crash of applause made her twitch as Kyle put her down.

Mr. Fisk was shaking his head. "Okay, okay, beautiful job, and I'll excuse the aerial out there since the agent's here, but no big lifts tomorrow."

He walked away, barking orders to Ado Annie to be

ready for her cue. Faith leaned against Kyle, trembling with nerves and excitement. "Oh my God, that was awesome."

He laughed and pulled her into a hug. "I hate how I have to look at you when I'm in character, but I have to admit, the lifts were pretty awesome."

"They were!" She gave him a quick kiss before bending down to pull off her pointe shoes. She'd have to "wake up" from her dream onstage soon. "Don't go anywhere—you have to take the curtain call with us."

He nodded, and she hustled back onstage, so full of joy, she might burst. And when the play was over, Kyle joined them onstage to applause. If Josh looked just a teeny bit sour, well, she couldn't be all that sorry.

The lights shone down on the ball field. It was a gorgeous spring night, warm with a soft breeze that teased summer's coming arrival. Graduation was coming, too, but Faith wasn't worried. Kyle's grandpa, who'd come to the musical on Kyle's ticket, had been pretty impressed. A week later, she was asked to send her audition to Elon in North Carolina. Apparently, one of the trustees was an old marine buddy, and they were considering her for a spot.

She fought a smile, thinking about how she and Kyle had celebrated the news, after he told her he'd follow her anywhere he could grow a garden.

"You look like a kitten sneaking a hot dog off the counter," Vi said, raising a brow. "Care to share?"

Faith blushed. "Uh, not really."

"Uh-huh, thought not." Vi winked, then looked down at the field. "I have to say, I do love those baseball pants. Nice view."

"Vi…"

"Hey, you can't say you haven't noticed."

No, she sure couldn't.

Faith sat up straighter as Kyle ran to the outfield. She waved, but he had that "I'm invincible" game face on, so all she could do was grin at Vi. "You ready?"

"I know nothing about this sport." Violet leaned back, putting her hands on the floor of the bleachers behind them. She wore a Suttonville T, ripped along the hem and tied around her waist. "Why's Kyle way out there?"

Faith laughed. "He's an outfielder. You know, in case someone hits a pop fly, he can catch it."

Vi stared at her, slack-jawed. "Are you speaking Swedish?"

Faith patted her shoulder. "You'll pick it up."

Alyssa sat on her other side. To Faith's surprise, she knew a lot about baseball. She was staring at the batter's box. "That guy from Midway has a terrible stance."

Terrible stance or not, the guy hit the ball pretty hard, and it sailed between Tristan and Kyle. They raced for it, and Kyle waved Tristan off, throwing himself out Superman-style to catch it. He landed on his chest and slid several feet before stopping and holding up his mitt, showing the ball to the umpire.

Kyle stood up and dusted himself off. There was a grass stain on his white jersey, but he was grinning when he went to give Tristan a fist bump. Faith stood and applauded, and that caught his eye. He blew her a kiss before moving back into position for the next batter.

"But the guy hit it," Vi protested. "He hit the stinking ball. Why's he out?"

"Because the Midway guy had a terrible stance," Alyssa said, as if that explained everything. "And because Faith's boyfriend is a badass."

Faith couldn't help but smile. Yeah, he was, but Kyle wasn't only a badass baseball player. He was kind, funny, and everything in between.

And most of all…he was hers.

Acknowledgments

This book fell onto the page—Faith and Kyle wanted their story told, and I loved every minute of telling it. That's a rare thing, as many stories require more effort than Faith's back yard. But every book requires more than just the author, and I have a lot of people to thank for helping it cross the finish line:

Heather Howland, my editor-extraordinaire, and the incredible staff at Entangled Teen for their advice, support, and general awesomeness.

Rodgers and Hammerstein for writing a musical about my home state—*Oklahoma!* is one of my favorites.

Sawyer Fredericks, whose song "Please" was the initial impetus for this story and for Kyle's character (Heather deserves all the credit for drawing it out), and Imagine Dragons's "The Fall" for helping me hear Faith for the first time.

My daughter Alex, to whom this book is dedicated, for all her help with voice. Having a built-in expert on the case was great. And to my son, Tanner, for teaching me how to use Snapchat, and actually friending me, too. I'm not sure how I got so lucky to have two incredible kids like you.

Finally, my husband, Ryan, for making sure I have space, time, and M&Ms for the journey. I couldn't do it without you.

About the Author

Kendra C. Highley lives in north Texas with her husband and two children. She also serves as staff to four self-important and high-powered cats. This, according to the cats, is her most critical job. She believes in everyday magic, extraordinary love stories, and the restorative powers of dark chocolate.

DARING THE BAD BOY
an *Endless Summer* novel by Monica Murphy

A session at summer camp is just what shy Annie McFarland needs to reinvent herself. Too bad her fear of water keeps her away from the lake, and her new crush Kyle. Enter Jacob Fazio—junior counselor, all-around bad boy, and most importantly: lifeguard. When a night of Truth or Dare gets him roped into teaching Annie how to swim, she begs him to also teach her how to snag Kyle. Late-night swim sessions turn into late-night kissing sessions…but there's more on the line than just their hearts. If they get caught, Jake's headed straight to juvie.

THE BOYFRIEND BET
a *Boyfriend Chronicles* novel by Chris Cannon

Zoe Cain knows that Grant Evertide, her brother's number-one nemesis, is way out of her league. So naturally, she kisses him. She's thrilled when they start dating, non-exclusively, but Zoe's brother claims Grant is trying to make her his "Ringer," an oh-so-charming tradition where a popular guy dates a non-popular girl until he hooks up with her, then dumps her. Zoe threatens to neuter Grant with hedge clippers if he's lying, but Grant swears he isn't trying to trick her. Still, that doesn't mean Grant is the commitment type—even if winning a bet is on the line.